the Buddha's Apprentice
at Bedtime

the Buddha's Apprentice at Bedtime

Tales of Compassion and Kindness for You to Read with Your Child – to Delight and Inspire

Dharmachari Nagaraja

WATKINS PUBLISHING

LONDON

The Buddha's Apprentice at Bedtime
Dharmachari Nagaraja

First published in the UK and USA in 2013 by
Watkins Publishing Limited
Sixth Floor
75 Wells Street
London W1T 3QH

A member of Osprey Group

Managing Editor: Sandra Rigby
Senior Editor: Fiona Robertson
Editor: Krissy Mallett
Managing Designer: Suzanne Tuhrim
Commissioned artwork: Sharon Tancredi (www.sharontancredi.com)

A CIP record for this book is available from the British Library

ISBN: 978-1-78028-514-6

10 9 8 7 6 5 4 3 2 1

Typeset in Cantoria MT
Colour reproduction by XY digital, UK
Printed in China

Distributed in the USA and Canada by
Sterling Publishing Co., Inc.
387 Park Avenue South
New York, NY 10016-8810

For information about custom editions, special sales, premium and corporate purchases, please contact Sterling Special Sales Department at 800-805-5489 or specialsales@sterlingpub.com.

A NOTE ON GENDER
In sections of this book intended for parents, to avoid burdening the reader repeatedly with phrases such as "he or she", "he" and "she" are used alternately, topic by topic, to refer to a child.

Contents

About This Book

Welcome to this new collection of Buddhist tales to share at bedtime with your children. It was wonderful to hear how many of you read and enjoyed my previous book, *Buddha at Bedtime*. This collection has also been inspired by the Jataka Tales – traditional stories offering wisdom and guidance which are believed to have been told by the Buddha himself. As in *Buddha at Bedtime*, the tales have been updated to make them both compelling and accessible for today's young reader.

The stories explore a wide range of characters and settings to help your child engage with the age-old truths they impart. They are focused around explaining the eight great principles that underpin Buddhism, known as the Eightfold Noble Path. A more detailed guide to these principles is provided later in the introduction, but in essence they give us a code of conduct for our daily lives: acting with kindness and compassion, speaking thoughtfully, earning our livelihoods in an ethical way and using the power of the mind to manage our thoughts.

Each story is based on one of the eight principles and draws out its key ideas. You will find, for example, the story of a nervous young horse who learns to control her anxious thoughts; a young boy who defeats a band of robbers by the power of meditation; a miser who learns that making money does not in itself create a happy life; and a spoilt duke's son who learns to speak thoughtfully and feel compassion for others.

The book's approach throughout is to encourage the understanding of an apprentice to the Buddha, a student who's learning the ways of the master.

The Jataka Tales are based on an ancient oral tradition where elders shared philosophical insights and powerful narratives at the conclusion of the day's work when their audience was calm, relaxed and ready to reflect on how they might best live their lives. By reading these stories aloud to your child at bedtime, you'll be drawing on the ancient power and wonder of the storytelling tradition. Taking the time to share the stories, to watch and respond to your child's reaction, and to encourage their imaginative exploration of characters and events, will help you both to unlock the rich wisdom underpinning each tale and highlight eternal truths for you to share.

You may also like to encourage your child to explore one of the key aspects of Buddhism, meditation. The stories can be a useful starting point in this process, helping to relax and calm your child. The introduction provides advice on incorporating meditation into your child's bedtime routine. You'll also find guided meditations inspired by the stories that you can do with your child at the back of the book.

Above all, enjoy the opportunity to share with your child the peace and understanding these simple yet profound Buddhist tales can awaken.

The Buddha and Buddhism

The timeless message of the Buddha continues to speak to
millions of people around the world. With its emphasis on
the reality of change in our lives, the importance of compassion
for others, and its focus on the management of the mind to avoid
unproductive anxiety and illusion, Buddhism seems in tune with
many of the insights of contemporary psychology and education.
For many it offers guidance on ethical and moral behaviour, as
well as practical assistance in coping with the stresses of day-to-
day living – skills that our children need now more than ever.

Buddhism is based on the teachings of the Buddha. The word
"Buddha" means "enlightened one" and reflects the great wisdom
the Buddha achieved in his lifetime. He began life as a privileged
Nepalese prince called Siddharta Gautama, born around 566 BC.
The oral traditions surrounding his life record that he grew
increasingly troubled by the suffering he saw beyond the palace
walls. He abandoned his position to search for an answer to the
misery he saw in daily life. The Buddha wandered
for years studying with wise men, living simply
and learning to meditate, but he was dissatisfied
with the answers to life's problems he encountered.
Finally the Buddha's enlightenment came as he
meditated beneath a bodhi tree.

He developed an understanding of life that
he came to call "The Four Noble Truths":

8

1. Everyone experiences suffering in life – no-one is exempt.
2. Suffering is caused by our focus on the material world – it is caused
by our greediness and constant desire for life to be more rewarding.
3. Suffering can be overcome.
4. The Eightfold Noble Path provides the guidance for overcoming suffering.

These truths formed the basis of the Buddha's new philosophy and he rapidly gained a group of followers who were inspired by his teachings. After the Buddha's death in around 486 BC these followers continued to develop the ideas he'd initiated. Buddhism began to spread throughout India and then into Nepal, Bhutan, China, Mongolia, Japan and Tibet.

In Tibet, the spreading of the wisdom of the Buddha was symbolized by the conch shell. The shell could be blown like a trumpet, sending the Buddha's words throughout the world.

Today Buddhism is one of the fastest-growing spiritual movements in the West. The teachings of Buddhism may seem deceptively simple but in fact are both subtle and complex. The tales in this collection aim to help the young reader explore how the Buddha's insights can help them in their daily life, just as Buddhism has helped millions of people around the world for thousands of years.

The Eightfold Noble Path

The essential principles of the Buddhist way of life are outlined in the Eightfold Noble Path. The Buddha himself described the Path as the means of overcoming suffering in life. The stories in this collection are based around these principles. Each one highlights ways to help your child understand each principle's meaning and truth. The eight principles can be grouped together in three main subjects: wisdom, ethics and concentration.

Wisdom

The great wisdom of the Buddha's ideas is symbolized in Tibetan Buddhism by an endless knot – his eternal wisdom, like the knot, has no beginning or end. Under the grouping of Wisdom we find two principles of the Path: *Right View* and *Right Intention*.

Right View centres on developing a deep understanding of the Four Noble Truths. There are two important aspects of Right View you can help your child to explore. Firstly, how everyone in the world experiences suffering, and secondly how suffering can be alleviated. The idea that everyone suffers may seem a harsh lesson, but it's the basis from which compassion and empathy then flow. The story of 'Tim and Grandpa Joe' illustrates how the kindness of Tim and his grandfather to the strangers they meet, as well as Tim's own kindness to his grandfather, is rewarded.

10

Right Intention helps us understand the importance of discipline and determination on the path to self-improvement. It focuses on how we need to make a commitment to self-improvement in order to grow and mature. The story of 'The Magic Moonlight Tree' is about a wise queen who shows another, less enlightened, ruler how to treat his subjects through her determination to save her people. Similarly, in the story 'Danan and the Serpent', Danan shows discipline and wisdom in order to save the lives of his siblings.

Ethics

The principles of the path we find under this grouping include *Right Speech*, *Right Action* and *Right Livelihood*.

Right Speech involves thinking about the impact of our speech on others. At a basic level this involves not lying and not speaking harshly or unkindly — and these are ideas most parents already work on with their children. At a deeper level, Right Speech asks us to speak thoughtfully, rather than thoughtlessly. In the story 'Egbert and the Fisherman', the rude young duke needs to learn to avoid the abusive, insensitive language he uses with his courtiers. Moreover, when he actually lies about the help he received from a poor fisherman, he's exposed before his people and nearly loses his dukedom. We see that the price of speaking thoughtlessly can be very high indeed.

Right Action asks us to behave morally and ethically with everyone we encounter in our daily lives. We must not harm others or steal from them. In the story of 'The New Girl' we discover how a bully, Hazel, learns the effect of her behaviour on others when she's magically turned into a rabbit – the self-same rabbit Hazel herself has hit with a slingshot. As she feels the rabbit's pain, Hazel vows never to act cruelly again.

Right Livelihood focuses on earning a living in a way that is ethical and doesn't involve harming other people. Children can be encouraged to think about the path that might inspire them in later life. In the story 'Ester and Lucky' we learn how a baby elephant, adopted by a childless woman, learns that life can be even more rewarding when she works productively, helping villagers cross a flooded river.

Concentration

The final three principles are *Right Mindfulness*, *Right Effort* and *Right Concentration*.

Right Mindfulness asks us to give our full attention to the present moment, simply observing what arises without judgment. It asks us to develop our concentration so that our mind can rise above the pettiness and distractions of daily life and learn true awareness. In 'Amrita and the Elephants', a young girl panics an entire village into believing the end of the world is approaching

– all through the power of her uncontrolled thoughts. Once her father gently calms her down, Amrita and the village realize that their fear was entirely the work of their overactive imagination.

Right Effort and *Right Concentration* involve focusing on the thoughts and actions that help us become more enlightened. These include compassion, kindness and gratitude. *Right Effort* involves the development of self-awareness. *Right Concentration* asks us to think about our behaviour and actively manage our thoughts so that we avoid thinking negatively about ourselves and others.

The Tibetan Buddhist symbol of the wheel symbolizes the interconnection between things and reminds us that our behaviour effects those around us and in turn, our karma.

For children, the aim is not to ask them to repress negative thoughts. Rather the idea is to get children to reflect on the meaning such thoughts might have. This is an idea explored in 'The Sheep Stealers'. Hamish may not have listened to his father's advice but he needed to forgive himself for his mistake.

In this book the moral at the end of each tale helps highlight the stage of the path the story explores. As you read it with your child, you may like to refer back to these pages to consider the implications of that stage of the path and discuss it together.

Working with the Stories

The oral storytelling tradition is rich in every culture. The Jataka Tales that inspire this collection are no different, having been loved by children and adults for thousands of years. Believed to have been created between 300 BC and 400 AD the tales are part of the canon of sacred Buddhist literature.

One of the first English translations of the tales was published by Edward Byles Cowell between 1895 and 1907. An illustrated children's edition was published in 1912 by Ellen C. Babbitt.

The tales comprise 550 anecdotes and fables, each one depicting an earlier incarnation of the Buddha. Sometimes he appears as an animal, sometimes as a human. The finest, most noble character in each story can be identified with the Buddha.

In this new collection, humour is often used to develop the story and captivate today's young reader. Strong characters and evocative settings will also help to draw your child into the narrative and help them relate to the action. But the essential purpose held by the original tales of developing the moral and ethical behaviour of the reader remains.

In some stories it will be easy to identify the Buddha. For example in 'The New Girl', the cruel Hazel learns an important lesson in compassion from Rosie, a girl whose very presence makes the school room light up and who has the power to transform Hazel into a rabbit. Clearly here is the Buddha in the form of a young girl.

In 'The Beautiful White Horse', the Buddha takes the form of a kindly squirrel who teaches the anxious horse how to calm her unquiet mind, while in 'The Magic Moonlight Tree', the queen of the monkeys is far wiser than the king who tries to capture her. The Buddha, this time in monkey form, explains what it takes to be a truly great ruler.

As you read the stories with your child you may like to explore with them the character that displays the greatest Buddha nature. Ask your child what it is that makes the character so wise and so generous and how the ideas presented might resonate in your child's daily life.

For example, most children will readily relate to the desire for a new toy explored in 'The Shiny Red Train', but will be drawn to think harder about how important possessions really are by the story's end. In 'The Spirit of the Tree', a child shows his parent how luck is not important – it's his father's own hard work that leads to his good fortune at the market. This in turn leads to interesting questions about how we can shape our own world by our attitudes and thoughts.

Enjoy the reading aloud experience with your child. Remember to read with enthusiasm and energy and slow down your pace so that your child has time to process the ideas raised by the stories. You'll reap the reward of a stimulating discussion and the developing awareness of your child.

Taking Buddhism Further

The stories in this collection aim to provide an accessible introduction for children to some of the key ideas of Buddhism. But there are other ways to encourage your child along the Buddhist path.

One possible starting point is to join a Buddhist community or *Sangha*. The concept of Sangha is considered to be one of the Three Jewels or Three Refuges of Buddhism, together with the Buddha himself, and *Dharma* or the path to enlightenment. Buddhism recognizes that joining a supportive community of like-minded people makes the journey to greater awareness easier, and so all Buddhists are encouraged to join a local group. In your own town or city you are likely to find a meditation group inspired by Buddhist teachings that you and your family will be welcome to join. Such groups are increasingly aware of the needs of children and offer play groups and other activities specifically designed for young people.

Your involvement in the community can take on many forms. You might like to volunteer to help with the cleaning and maintenance of the premises, to join in festivals and celebrations or to attend classes. All forms of participation will be beneficial in helping you develop relationships with others on the same path. There are also traditional Buddhist practices that you and your child might enjoy exploring.

For instance, in the Tibetan Buddhist tradition, prayer flags
– rectangular pieces of brightly coloured cloth – are strung around
temples. Traditionally the flags are printed with a horse carrying
the Three Jewels. They also bear mantras, or sacred chants. The
concept behind the flag is that as it blows in the wind its message
of peace and compassion will spread throughout the world.

You might like to develop this idea with your child in your
own home. Together, write some messages of peace and love on
pieces of cloth and tie them to a tree in your garden. If you don't
have a garden you could tie positive messages to the tail of a kite
and fly it with your child in a local park, letting the wind spread
your thoughts of love and kindness.

Colouring in mandalas is another practice that you can
introduce to your child. Mandalas are symbolic geometric
designs. They're traditionally used in Buddhism to aid
concentration and meditation as they provide a focus for the
mind. Many people work with stencils of mandalas and colour
them in with paints, crayons or pencils. The act of colouring in
is powerfully meditative in itself and the end result is a beautiful
piece of art that you might like to frame and hang on the wall
as a further meditation tool. For your child this will be a fun
introduction to meditative techniques. Books of mandala stencils
are readily available and you'll find hundreds of designs from
which to choose.

Introducing Meditation

One of the key elements of Buddhism is developing the practice of meditation. Meditation teaches us many important and valuable skills. We learn to calm our minds, we learn to disengage from the dramas and distractions of the day, and we discover a still place from where we can achieve a new level of awareness. Working with the ideas in this book is an easy and enjoyable way to introduce meditation to your child.

You can incorporate meditation into your child's bedtime routine – either instead of or after reading one of the stories in this book, which have a powerful meditative quality themselves in that they focus your child's attention and encourage him to visualize settings, characters and events.

Meditation will calm your child before bed. In time he can learn to do the practice by himself whenever he's feeling anxious, but at first try to set aside five to ten minutes each day in which to do a guided meditation (see pages 120–123). You may also like to try the relaxation exercise on pages 118–9 beforehand.

Initially it'll be useful to explain the concept of meditation as going on an adventure of discovery. This will encourage your child to be open to and to work with whatever unfolds. But it's important to ensure that he feels safe and that he knows that he can stop at any time if he becomes uncomfortable or tired.

By teaching your child how to consciously meditate, you'll bring deep contentment and focus into his everyday life.

The Art of Storytelling

Your child may like to read these stories by herself, but as the stories originate from an oral storytelling tradition there will be a great deal of benefit in reading the stories aloud. Reading aloud enables you to share insights with your child, to explore hidden meanings and relate the characters and events to daily life.

Before you begin reading aloud, read through the stories yourself so that you can read with confidence and expression. You don't need to put yourself under great pressure – just enjoy the experience, reading slowly and allowing time for your child to comment on the characters and events. It's important that you are relaxed and focused on the reading, so try and spend a few minutes taking some deep breaths and stretching any tense muscles before you start.

Make sure that your child, too, is calm and ready to listen. The stories will in themselves have a calming effect but it'll be very helpful to also encourage your child to take some deep breaths and to relax her body so that she is comfortable. You might even like to do the relaxation exercise described on pages 118–9 to ensure your child is fully relaxed.

Each story ends with an idea to help your child unravel the meaning of the tale. Take time to discuss these with your child and explore her thoughts and feelings about them. There is no better way to ensure a refreshing night's sleep for your child than to calmly reflect together on the wise insights of the Buddha.

Bella and the Magic Soup

Relax, close your eyes and imagine a little girl called Bella who was always getting distracted. One day she was made responsible for a very special task, but she almost forgot to do it. Would you like to know what it was? Listen carefully to her story.

It had rained heavily all night as Bella slept. When she woke the next morning the sun was shining and the whole world sparkled. Bella jumped out of bed and ran to the window. The sunlight flew in and tickled her toes.

"It's such a lovely day, I must get outside," Bella thought to herself. She dressed very quickly and jumped down the stairs two at a time. But just as her hand reached for the front door knob, her mother, Mrs Button, called out: "Bella! I need help in the kitchen."

In the kitchen Mrs Button was wrestling with a big soup pot, trying to get its lid on. Just when she thought she had got it on securely, the lid sprang off into the air!

"Bella, can you get me some string?" asked Mrs Button.

Bella went to a drawer and found some string and handed it to her mother.

"I'm making magic soup," said Mrs Button. "It's got a lot of pepper in it and a lot of magic, and it's so powerful it's making the pot sneeze."

"Ah-choo!" cried the pot and the lid flew through the air. Mrs Button caught it and, quick as a flash, she got it back on the pot and tied it down with the string.

"Phew, what a bother!" she said, wiping her brow. "Now Bella, I've made this special magic soup for Granny. She's had a small accident."

Tears sprang into Bella's eyes, but her mother reassured her quickly. "Granny's all right. She just slipped over while she was doing some work in the garden. I want you to take her this Bumps and Bruises Cure Soup to help her get better," said Mrs Button.

"Poor Granny Button," replied Bella. "I'll take the soup to her right away."

Bella rushed out of the kitchen and through the front door and was halfway down the path before she realized she had forgotten the soup.

"You'd forget your own head if it wasn't stuck on," said her mother, smiling. She handed Bella the pot of soup.

"Now, concentrate and take this straight to Granny's house, and no dilly-dallying on the way," said Mrs Button.

22

"Yes, Mum," replied Bella as she clutched the soup.

Bella headed for her granny's house, but soon she was feeling rather hot. It was hard work carrying the heavy pot of soup, especially as it kept sneezing.

Bella stopped in the middle of a field of flowers and, putting the pot on the ground, she peeled off her coat.

"Phew, that's better," thought Bella.

Just then a breeze rustled the flowers, and a beautiful cloud of butterflies rose into the sky.

Bella clapped her hands in delight and danced after them as they fluttered away. She didn't notice as the pot sneezed again and bounced off into the long grass.

A big red butterfly landed on Bella's nose and tickled her. She sneezed and that reminded her about the soup pot. She ran back to where she had left it, but it was gone! Bella searched everywhere, but the pot was nowhere to be seen. Hot, bothered and upset, she sat down and began to cry.

Her crying woke a caterpillar from his afternoon nap.

"Young lady, why are you so upset?" asked the caterpillar. "Can I help?"

"My granny hurt herself and I was taking her some soup. Only I got distracted and I put down the pot, and now it's gone and it's all my fault," sobbed Bella.

"There now, don't cry," said the caterpillar. "I'm low to the ground and see everything. I'll find your pot."

And sure enough, after a little while the caterpillar called out to Bella, "I spy with my little eye something beginning with 'P'."

"Pot?" asked Bella hopefully.

Just then the pot gave an extra large sneeze and flew into the air. Bella ran and caught it before it could fall back into the long grass.

"Thank you, Caterpillar," said Bella. "I'm off to Granny's house now and nothing is going to distract me this time."

"Right you are," said the caterpillar. "Oh, look out!"

Bella had set off again, but almost walked into a tree.

"That was close!" Bella thought, "I need to concentrate while I'm looking around."

The beautiful cloud of butterflies wafted around her but this time Bella didn't get distracted. She came to a wood where some of her friends were laughing, climbing trees and swinging from the branches. They called out to her but Bella kept her eyes on the path. Although she longed to go and join the fun, she called out, "I can't play today, I'm busy." She concentrated on what she had to do, and wasn't bothered by her friends' teasing.

Bella's best friend, Daisy, ran after her.

"Wait!" She called. "I have pocket money. Mum says I can buy ice cream. Do you want to come with me?"

Bella's mouth began to water. An ice cream would have been so lovely. But she remembered her poor granny and held on to the soup pot firmly. "I would if I could, but I can't, thank you," she replied.

With a rumbling tummy, Bella finally made it to her granny's house. Granny ate all the magic Bumps and Bruises Cure Soup and was soon feeling much better.

When she'd finished, Granny put a large bowl of Bella's favourite chocolate-chip ice cream in front of her and poured her a tall glass of homemade lemonade.

"There you are, Bella," said Granny. "That's my gift to you in return for your kindness in bringing me the soup."

Bella smiled. Knowing she'd helped to make her granny well again was the best reward she could have had.

It's easy to get distracted and not finish something we've started. Try to concentrate on what you have to do and remember that other people may be counting on you.

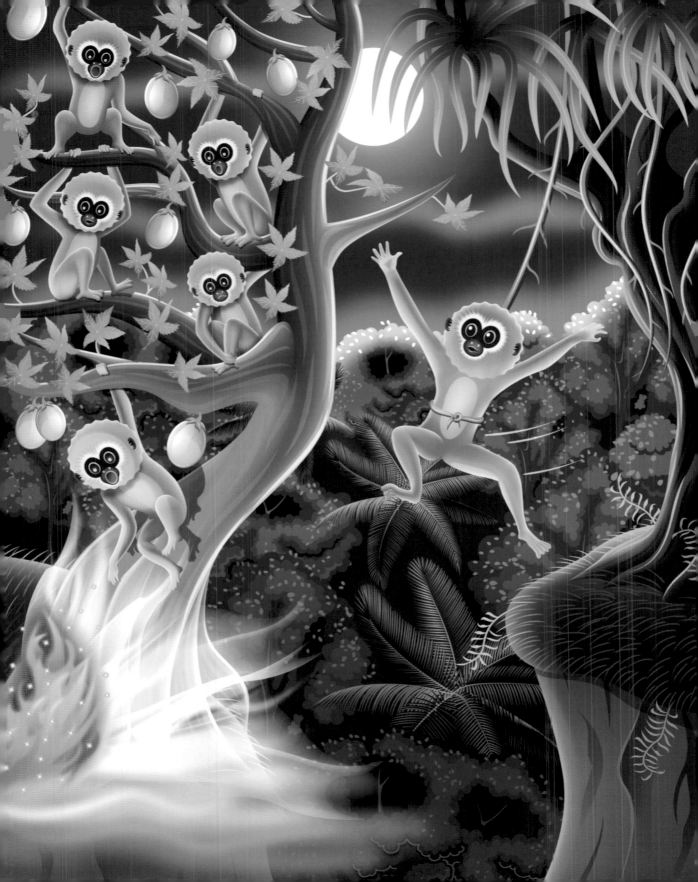

The Magic
Moonlight Tree

Relax, close your eyes and picture yourself in a steamy tropical jungle. This tale is about two young gibbons called Ginger and Snapp, who one day made a great discovery. Would you like to know what it was? Listen carefully to their story.

"Wow!" exclaimed Ginger. The two gibbons were staring up open-mouthed at an enormous tree, unlike any they'd seen before. The majestic tree stood on the edge of a deep ravine. Its leaves were vivid blue and shaped like stars and its branches were heavy with shiny oval fruits the colour of a silvery moon.

Ginger reached up and a fruit came free with a "pop!" Ginger and Snapp sniffed at it curiously.

"Do you think it's poisonous?" asked Snapp.

"I don't know," said Ginger. "It smells delicious."

"I think we should take it to Queen Echa," Snapp suggested. "She knows absolutely everything. She'll be able to tell us if it's safe to eat."

Queen Echa lived high on a mountainside in a tree that was so tall it reached above the clouds. The wise queen gasped when Ginger and Snapp gave her the mysterious fruit. "I've heard of this fruit. I don't know its name, but I believe that, once upon a time, it grew everywhere in our land. Then the humans came. They ate all the fruit and chopped down all the trees to build houses."

"That was selfish and very silly," said Ginger.

"I'm afraid humans aren't very smart," said Queen Echa sadly.

She shared the fruit with Ginger and Snapp. It was the most scrumptious food they'd ever tasted.

Queen Echa wanted to share the wonderful fruit with all her subjects. She asked Ginger and Snapp to lead her and a large party of gibbons down to the extraordinary tree.

When they reached it, Queen Echa solemnly hugged the tree and whispered: "We'll take only a little of your precious fruit now and we'll spread the seeds throughout the forest. In that way your family can flourish once again."

The tree seemed to shake with delight as the gibbons clambered among its branches gathering the silver fruit.

Suddenly a trumpet blasted and all the gibbons froze. The forest fell silent. Another trumpet blast, closer this time, mingled with voices and the "clip-clop" of horses' hooves.

"Humans!" said Queen Echa softly. "Everyone be still." The gibbons watched a procession led by King Barnabas pass right under the tree. Just then, a ripe fruit "popped" and dropped in front of King Barnabas. He came to a halt. He looked down at the fruit and then up into the tree. He saw the frightened faces of dozens of gibbons looking back at him. As the king and his men dismounted to investigate the fruit, the gibbons scrambled higher into the tree.

"Can I eat it or is it poisonous?" the king asked.

The king's taster took a small bite and declared it safe to eat and utterly delicious.

"What a great day," proclaimed the king. "We have discovered a tasty new fruit and a tree full of gibbons. We shall eat well tonight. Set fires around the tree and smoke out the apes." His men went quickly to do his bidding.

Queen Echa had to act fast. She raced along a branch that hung out over the ravine, launched herself into the air and flew across. As she landed on the other side she grabbed a long vine attached to a nearby tree. She tied the loose end around her waist, then threw herself back across the ravine to the fruit tree. But the vine was just a little too short and Queen Echa could only catch the tip of the branch. She held on tightly as Ginger and Snapp ran to her aid. The other gibbons looked on horrified. Without a care for her own safety, Queen Echa called to Ginger and Snapp:

"Gather the others quickly and use me as a bridge. Get to safety."

"The humans will catch you!" they cried.

"Don't argue. Do what I say!" ordered the queen. Ginger and Snapp rushed back into the tree and instructed all the gibbons to escape. They clambered across the queen's back and along the vine to the safety of the other side of the ravine.

All this time the king's men were busy collecting more wood to add to the fires. When King Barnabas shouted out that the gibbons were escaping, his captain strung his bow and took aim at Queen Echa's heart.

"Stop, don't shoot!" ordered the king. "I want you to bring me that gibbon, and treat her gently."

The captain climbed into the tree and brought Queen Echa before the king. He expected her to quake with fear but instead she just smiled.

"Why are you smiling?" asked King Barnabas.

"My subjects are all free and safe. That's all that matters. If you want to be a good ruler you must put the lives of others before your own."

King Barnabas was stunned by her words and bowed his head in respect. "You're a noble and selfless queen. You've taught me a great lesson today. I'm humbled."

King Barnabas was so moved by Queen Echa's selfless behaviour that he made a royal decree: "I hereby state that, from this day forth, this tree and all its fruits are to be protected from harm."

To celebrate, the humans and gibbons sat together around the tree and had a great feast. Queen Echa asked Ginger and Snapp to present the king with seeds from the oval fruits so that he might grow his own trees.

The king was so delighted he made another pronouncement: "This fruit, which has no name we know of, will from this day be called, 'Queen Echa fruit'."

All the king's men and all the gibbons, but especially Ginger and Snapp, cheered very loudly indeed.

Acting selflessly in the interests of others is one of the noblest things you can do. If you act in a kind and considerate way, everyone around you will benefit.

The New Girl

Relax, close your eyes and picture the toughest, meanest kid in school. This story is about Hazel, a little girl who frightened everybody until one day the most incredible thing happened to her. Listen carefully to her story.

"She's coming!" cried Tiny running back to his seat. The classroom fell ominously silent as the door flew open. It wasn't the teacher who scared the children. It was a girl called Hazel Nutt. Some said she'd been bullied when she was small. Others said she was born mean. But most people just tried to keep out of her way. The only time Hazel smiled was when she made someone cry.

Miss Poppy, the teacher, came in behind Hazel. She was just sitting down when there was a knock at the door and another girl walked in. As she entered the room the sun came out and seemed to fall on the floor before her.

"I'm Rosie Peach," she said. "I'm the new girl."

For the rest of that day the atmosphere in the classroom was light and happy, as if a shadow had lifted. Rosie's smile

33

was infectious to all except Hazel Nutt, who was feeling something she didn't often feel. She felt frightened.

The final bell rang. Shoving away everyone in her path, Hazel went to the nearby forest and angrily pulled out her catapult. "I need some cheering up," she said to herself.

Hazel spied a rabbit sunning itself in a pool of light. Quick as a flash she loaded her catapult with a stone, took aim and fired. The stone hit the rabbit on the thigh. The animal jumped in fright and Hazel ran after it, laughing. Then she stopped dead. There was Rosie, sitting in the grass, stroking the rabbit and singing to it. The rabbit's leg was bleeding.

"You give me that rabbit. It's mine!" yelled Hazel.

"This rabbit belongs to itself," said Rosie. "It's wild."

"It's just a dumb animal," laughed Hazel. "Are you a bit stupid? You talk to animals do you?"

"Yes, as a matter of fact, I do. Come closer and listen yourself." Rosie hummed softly to the rabbit.

"Is this a trap?" thought Hazel. She moved closer, ready to fight if she had to. "I can't hear anything," she said.

"Closer, come closer," said Rosie.

One of Rosie's hands was resting on the rabbit's wound. As Hazel lent forward, Rosie's other hand shot up and touched Hazel on her chest over her heart. Hazel froze. The world started spinning. She wanted to jump and laugh. She also wanted to eat grass! What was happening to her?

34

A sharp pain bit into her thigh and she screamed. Her leg was bleeding. A girl was running toward her with a catapult. Hazel could make no sense of it. She limped into the undergrowth. The pain was terrible. Then she saw Rosie, sitting on the grass and singing. She laid her head in the girl's lap and, as Rosie gently stroked her, the pain began to ease.

Rosie took her hand from Hazel's heart.

"What did you do to me?" sobbed Hazel.

"I let you see and feel what this little rabbit saw and felt as you hurt it," said Rosie.

"I'm so sorry." Hazel stroked the rabbit. Then she took it home and cared for it until it was better. From then on, Hazel was no longer a frightening, angry girl. Soon, everyone wanted to be her friend. And no-one noticed that Rosie, the new girl, didn't come back to school. In some ways it seemed as if Hazel was the new girl now.

*Sometimes we might act tough, to hide the
frightened or confused way we feel inside.
Trying to see the other person's point of view
can help us to understand and be kind to each other.*

35

Ester and Lucky

Relax, close your eyes and picture Ester, an old woman who many years ago had been a celebrated acrobat but now earned her meagre living telling tales about the circus. One night she had a special delivery that was to change her life for ever. Would you like to know what happened? Listen carefully to her story.

Ester was sitting alone by the fire when there was a loud "knock, knock" at the front door. "Who can be calling at this time of night?" she wondered. She opened the door, but no-one was there. Then she took a step back in surprise.

On the doorstep was a large basket with a baby elephant inside! Ester dragged the basket into the house. The little elephant was sleeping soundly wrapped in a blanket.

"Well, my horoscope said I'd receive an unexpected delivery. This must be it!" she chuckled, smiling at the sleeping baby elephant. "I'll call her 'Lucky'," she said.

Ester never worried why Lucky had been left on her doorstep. Lucky just needed someone to care for her –

and that is what Ester did. There was not much money in circus tales, so Ester took in washing and did any little jobs that would help feed Lucky. Lucky grew into a very happy little elephant. Every day she swam with the local children in the pools under the waterfalls in the forest. They shared lemonade and ice cream, picnicking among the ancient, moss-covered trees.

In autumn, Lucky and the children played chase among the fallen leaves. When winter rolled out a carpet of snow, they built snow elephants. Then the air grew warmer and spring brought forth buds on the trees. Many years passed in this way and soon Lucky was a fully grown elephant.

One day Lucky said to Ester, "Come to the woods today. You're looking tired. I'm sure the walk will do you good."

"But I must go to work," replied Ester. "If I don't work there's no money, and if there's no money there's no food."

Lucky hadn't realized that Ester's storytelling wasn't just for fun. Or that all that washing was to get money to buy food. She looked at Ester and saw for the first time that she'd grown old. "I'm young and strong," Lucky thought. "I've had plenty of playing. Now I must make time to work."

Lucky decided to find some work to earn money. She had no idea what she could do, but she headed off along the river to ask the people in next village if she could help.

Heavy rains had washed away the bridge to the village, but Lucky calmly waded through the waters. She was met by a cheering crowd of villagers. Since the flood they'd had to travel far upriver to find a safe crossing place.

The mayor said: "Great elephant, we'll pay you a silver piece each time you help us to cross the river."

"Happy to help," said a delighted Lucky. She enjoyed chatting to the villagers as she carried them. At the end of the day the mayor gave her a pouch full of silver pieces.

When she got home, Lucky gave Ester the silver.

"Now you can stay home and I'll work," said Lucky, pleased that her work had made so many people happy.

From that day forth Lucky worked and Ester stayed at home. When Lucky had finished her day's work, they'd sit in the garden and Ester would tell stories of the circus – just for the fun of it.

Working might not sound like much fun, but try doing work that helps other people as well as yourself – you may find you have even more fun than when you're playing!

The Shiny
Red Train

Relax, close your eyes and imagine that you live with all your family in a tiny shack on a cold and windy beach. This story is about Michael, a little boy whose family was very poor. All his clothes were old and ragged and his toys had all been found on the beach. More than anything, Michael wanted a new toy. Listen carefully to his story.

One day, he and his sister Claire visited the town's toy shop, just to look at the toys. Michael found the most beautiful toy train he had ever seen.

"Put it back," said Claire. She tried to wrestle the shiny red train from her brother's grip.

"But I want it!" protested Michael.

"We haven't got any money," replied Claire firmly. She managed to prize the train from his hands and Michael burst into tears. Everyone in the shop stared at them. Claire grabbed her brother's hand and pulled him toward the door, knocking down a pile of stripy hula hoops. Everyone laughed as the children ran out the door.

Michael cried all the way home. His family's beach shack was built from the bones of an enormous whale. Its walls were made of driftwood and the roof was made from pieces of plastic sheeting that had washed up on the beach. Claire loved their home, but Michael hated it. He wanted to live in a proper house. And he hated his old broken toys from the beach. His father fixed them as best he could, but they were not the same as new toys.

Michael went to bed that night feeling very sorry for himself. He couldn't stop thinking about the shiny red train he'd held in the toy shop that day. He wanted it so much, more than anything else in the world. Finally he fell asleep.

Michael opened his eyes. He was standing in the toy shop with Claire, but this time the whole place seemed to be alive! Toy cars beeped and flashed their lights at him, and trains shot past on invisible tracks. Teddy bears laughed and jumped from shelf to shelf and dolls twirled in their dresses.

"Could this be a dream?" Michael wondered, but everything was so real. Bright kites flew above his head and, when Michael looked up, the ceiling itself looked like the night sky, aglow with hundreds of little lights that twinkled like stars.

"It must be magic," Michael thought.

The shop door chimed as customers came and went, loaded with bags and boxes.

The cash register drawer flew open as the shopkeeper, Mrs Holly, rang up sale after sale.

Everyone looked full of joy. Michael felt happy too. On a cabinet right in front of him stood the shiny red train. It tooted at him and Michael reached out and touched it.

Claire pulled at his sweater. "Let's try the lucky dip."

"I want the red train," Michael said.

"But we haven't enough money, I told you that already," she replied. "We've got enough for the lucky dip, though."

Claire gave Mrs Holly the money for the lucky dip and thrust her hand into the bucket piled high with brightly coloured packages. "Oh! A beautiful doll!" cried Claire as she unwrapped her present.

When no-one was looking, Michael grabbed the red train and hid it under his sweater. As he did so, the bright lights of the shop faded and the teddy bears stopped laughing. With Claire close behind, Michael hurried to the door and plunged into the crowd of shoppers.

It was dark and cold outside. Michael pulled out the shiny train from under his sweater.

Claire began to cry. "You stole it," she said.

"I don't care," Michael replied. His voice was cold and hard. "I wanted it."

"But it belongs to Mrs Holly," said Claire.
"Well, it's mine now. She has plenty of toys."
Michael walked down to the sea where the
moon was shining brightly on the waves. He was
admiring the way his train glittered in the moonlight,
but then he spied a woman walking along the shore.
He hid the train under his sweater again. As
the woman came closer, he saw she was crying
and scattering bows and wrapping paper into the sea.
Michael realized it was Mrs Holly.

"Why are you throwing away all your wrapping paper?"
Michael asked her. He felt frightened.

"I've no need of it now," Mrs Holly said, sadly. "Little
boys and girls come to my lovely shop and take my toys.
If you don't pay for them, I've no money to pay my bills.
Today the landlord took my shop away." She began to sob.
"I don't know how I'll feed my children."

The train hidden under Michael's sweater felt hot.
It was so hot it was like an ache next to his heart.
Michael was ashamed. He understood now how
selfish he had been. He pulled out the shiny red
train and handed it to Mrs Holly.

"I'm sorry, please forgive me."

As Mrs Holly took the train, rainbow-coloured puffs of
smoke belched from its funnel and its whistle tooted loudly.

The train shot joyfully into the night sky, leaving a trail of sparkly stars behind it before returning to Mrs Holly's arms.

The shopkeeper smiled as she leaned forward and kissed Michael on the forehead.

Suddenly, Michael was dazzled by morning sunlight. He saw above him the whale bones holding up the roof. He was in his own bed. "It must have been a dream!" he laughed.

Several weeks later Michael walked through the door of the toy shop. He went straight up to the counter and gave Mrs Holly all the money he'd saved from doing little jobs for the people of the town.

"May I please buy the shiny red train?" he asked her.

"Of course, Michael," smiled Mrs Holly.

As he walked out of the shop with his train wrapped in a big ribbon, Mrs Holly called after him: "Thank you, Michael." She winked at him. And Michael smiled back.

Doing the right thing means not being selfish, however unfair life seems to be. It can be painful not to have all the things other people have, but we can always be grateful for what we do have.

The Sheep Stealers

Relax, close your eyes and imagine that you live on a sheep farm in the Scottish highlands. This story is about two young brothers, Hamish and Dougal Woolly. One day their father had an accident and the two boys had to grow up fast. Listen carefully to their story.

"Oooops!" cried Mr Woolly. Hamish and Dougal rushed out to the farmyard to find their father on the ground, clutching his ankle. "I slipped off the ladder," he explained. "And now I can't stand up!"

The boys carried their father indoors. "You boys are going to have to take the sheep to market," said Mr Woolly. "Use the ferry to cross the river. The forest is too dangerous."

"But Father, that'll take twice the time!" protested Hamish. "I'm not frightened of the forest."

"Well, you should be! There are thieves and dangerous animals and I won't be there to protect you. I want you to go by the river and no argument about it," said Mr Woolly.

The boys rounded up the sheep and set out the next morning. When they reached the river there was no ferry to be seen. The boys waited and waited but no-one came.

"Let's go through the forest," said Hamish. "It's much less effort."

"But Father said it wasn't safe," said Dougal.

"Father worries too much," replied Hamish.

In the end Hamish stormed off to the forest, taking half the sheep with him. "See you at the market!" he called.

Dougal sat with the remaining sheep wondering how to cross the river. "Perhaps I could make some stepping stones," he thought, but the rocks he threw into the water sank out of sight. Then he built a raft but that sank, too.

"Those ideas didn't work, but I'll keep trying," he said. He toiled all day, but with no success. When it got dark he went to sleep, trusting the answer would be clearer in the morning.

By contrast, Hamish had a lazy day leading his sheep through the forest. When night fell, he lay down to sleep under a tree, full of confidence. "I'll show Dougal," he said.

In the forest, a gang of sheep rustlers led by Fingers the wolf had followed Hamish's progress all day. In the dead of night Fingers, and his two mean-looking foxes, spirited away the sheep to their den.

"We'll get a fine price for these sheep," Fingers said.

Down by the river, the morning sun woke Dougal. "Got it!" he suddenly exclaimed. He climbed up to a tall tree and began chopping at its base with his axe. The tree fell right across the river forming a bridge for the sheep to cross.

In the forest Hamish woke to find all his sheep had gone. He searched and searched, but could find no trace of them. "I've let everyone down," he thought sadly as he began his long, lonely walk home. "And we badly needed the money."

Two days later Dougal arrived at the market and sold his sheep for a handsome profit. When he arrived home, his parents and Hamish were waiting to welcome him. Hamish looked so forlorn his father gave him a hug. "The most important thing is that we're all safe and together again, but I hope you've learned a lesson," said Mr Woolly to Hamish. "There are no shortcuts. Success takes hard work."

The easiest solution to a problem isn't always the best one – it can take a lot of effort and hard thinking to reach your goals. Help yourself by following advice from more experienced people.

Aloka and the Band of Robbers

Relax, close your eyes and picture yourself deep in a jungle in Thailand, far from the nearest village. This story is about a clever boy called Aloka, who was sent away from his village to study in the great temple of Golden City. One day he was walking home to his village for the holidays when he met a band of robbers! Would you like to find out what happened? Listen carefully to his story.

Night was drawing in as Aloka made his way along the jungle trail. Ferns and palm trees lined the path and vines climbed into the sky. He was preparing to camp for the night when he met a family of merchants returning from market.

"Why don't you camp with us tonight?" said Taai, the father of the family.

"Yes, come and share our meal," said Rajini, his wife.

Aloka smiled gratefully. He had been walking for several days on his own and was very glad to have some company. He joined the family around a blazing camp fire and shared a delicious meal with them.

After they'd all eaten their fill, Taai put more logs on the fire. Then his six children gathered around to listen to him tell a story.

"Once upon a time there was a young Prince called Siddartha," began Taai. "Although he was very rich and handsome, he was not happy. Siddartha could see that many people in his kingdom suffered. He wanted to help them but he didn't know how, until one day he found the secret. Now children, do you know what that secret was?"

The youngest child, little Mai, spoke up. "The power to be happy is in your own mind," she said.

"Very good, Mai," said her father. "That's exactly what the prince learned. Once he could control his mind through meditation, nothing had the power to frighten or upset him. He could help people, because he was at peace. And he taught people how they could help themselves."

The children listened to Prince Siddartha's adventures. They'd all heard the story many times before, but they loved it just the same. A large silver moon climbed into the night's sky and Taai's gentle voice lulled the family into sleep. Then Taai himself closed his eyes and began to snore softly.

But young Aloka was wide awake. He was very excited by Prince Siddartha's story. Now everything he'd learned at school about controlling his mind seemed to make sense.

Aloka wrapped himself in a blanket and walked over to a nearby fig tree where he would not disturb the family. He wanted to think about the ideas calmly and walked slowly back and forth in the cool night air. As he let his attention focus on his breathing, his mind began to settle. Aloka's teacher at the temple had taught him to do this whenever he got over-excited. Now he felt calm and at peace.

What Aloka did not know was that he and the family were in terrible danger. A band of robbers had spied the family's camp fire from afar and quietly made their way through the jungle. Now they were hiding behind a boulder, watching Aloka and the sleeping family.

"Look at that family all fast asleep," whispered their leader, Cha. "It'd be easy to steal from them."

"Yes, and they're just back from market from the looks of it," said his deputy, Jao. "Look at all those bundles of cloth."

The family all slept on peacefully. Now Aloka spied the robbers but he decided to remain calm, as he'd been taught. "It'll do no good if I panic," he thought to himself. "I'll try to control my fear." He continued to walk slowly back and forth under the tree, practising concentration.

"That man pacing there must be on guard," said Bahn, the third robber. "Let's wait until he falls asleep."

"And then we can tie up the adults and take everything they own!" said Jao. "I've the ropes ready."

The robbers waited for Aloka to go to sleep. They waited and they waited, but Aloka continued to walk back and forth under the tree. One by one, Cha, Jao and Bahn fell into fitful sleep. Every now and then, one of them would stir and open his eyes. But when he saw that Aloka was still awake, each robber would fall asleep once more. Finally, when the sun rose in the sky, all three robbers woke up.

"That guard is still awake!" growled Cha. "And now it's daylight. It's too risky for us to try to rob them now. They'll wake up before we have a chance to tie them up."

The angry robbers fled through the jungle as the morning light flooded into the valley. Jao was so annoyed he forgot to take his ropes with him. The leader, Cha, couldn't resist calling out, "Hey, you lot, sleeping there without a care in the world! You were lucky this time. Your guard who never sleeps saved you! You should reward him well."

Aloka watched them leave and at last stopped walking. He stretched his arms and legs and smiled quietly to himself. Soon everyone was up and bustling about preparing breakfast. Taai began gathering wood for a fire and found the trampled-down patch of ferns where the robbers had hidden. And then he discovered the ropes.

"Aloka, do you know how these got here?" asked Taai. He was concerned and confused.

"Oh yes, they belonged to the robbers who were watching our camp during the night. They left this morning," replied Aloka calmly.

"Robbers!" cried Taai. "Weren't you scared?"

"No," said Aloka. "I felt very peaceful as I walked. I realized that robbers are only interested in rich people. I'd only my blanket and a calm mind and neither would be of interest to robbers. So why should I be afraid?"

"You're very brave," said Taai. "Because you remained calm in the face of danger, danger passed us all by."

The family walked with Aloka back to his village. When they reached Aloka's home, Taai met Aloka's father and bowed to him. He told him the story of the robbers.

"Your son is the wisest young man I know," Taai said. "You should be very proud."

Aloka's father smiled and nodded. "I am," he said.

Right concentration or meditation is about training your heart and mind. Once you're calm and at peace, bravery and wisdom will come naturally to you.

The Monkey Thieves

Relax, close your eyes and picture a band of very naughty monkeys. Every night the monkeys would creep into the King's orchard and steal his delicious apricots, plums and peaches. Would you like to know what happened? Listen carefully to their story.

The head gardener stood before the King in the great throne room of the palace. "I'm sorry Your Majesty," he said. "We laid traps and nets but these monkeys are slippery devils. They got away again last night."

"We must try to solve this problem together," replied the King. "Remember, I don't want to hurt the monkeys, I just want to stop them eating my fruit."

There was silence in the throne room as all the King's staff thought hard. Finally Buttercup, the cook's daughter, came forward and bowed to the King. "Your Majesty, doesn't eating fruit make you fit and healthy?"

"Yes, I believe it does, Buttercup," said the King.

"I like fruit, but I love cake," Buttercup continued.

"But when I eat too much cake my tummy feels heavy and sometimes I even feel sleepy."

"Yes, I also feel tired if I eat too much cake," laughed the King, "but I don't get your meaning."

"If you could tempt the monkeys to eat a lot of cake, they would become sleepy. Then they wouldn't be able to run so fast and they might be easier to catch," explained Buttercup.

"And Your Majesty," added Basil, the son of the King's shoemaker, "we've all noticed how vain these monkeys are. They love anything bright and sparkling, and they steal jewelry and bright clothing. I've seen them hang necklaces around their necks and bangles from their arms. I've even seen them trying on shoes!"

"That's all very well," said the King, "but I don't see how that helps us to catch those rascals."

"I can create the most beautiful pairs of sparkling high-heeled shoes that the monkeys won't be able to resist," Basil continued. If their tummies are full with cake and they are wearing high-heeled shoes they'll never escape us."

At first the King just laughed at these plans. But when the monkeys continued to steal his fruit for the next three nights in a row, he was ready to give anything a try.

He ordered his finest pastry chefs to create the most delicious array of cakes. The cooks spent an entire day whipping cream, mixing chocolate sauce and spinning sugar.

By late afternoon they were ready to lay
out an enormous, mouth-watering spread on a
huge cake stand in the middle of the orchard. The stand
groaned under the weight of cream-filled cupcakes, iced
buns, chocolate sponges, cherry pies and apricot tarts.
The wonderful aroma floated over the orchard.

Meanwhile Basil was creating the most beautiful
monkey shoes that had ever been seen. When they
were finished he hung them from the branches
of the trees in the orchard. The trap was set.
The King's guards hid among the trees and waited.

As afternoon wore on toward evening,
the monkey thieves crept through the trees.

"Mmm, what is that delicious smell?"
asked Snout.

"It's cake! I love cake!" cheered Lugs and Peeper.

"Stay still," hissed Wit. "This could be a trap.
We should leave and come back another time."

"We don't like it either! It all feels a bit
suspicious," said Gob and Peck. But no-one
made a move to leave. Everyone was too
busy staring at the cream cakes and tarts.
The more they stared at the yummy delicacies,
the harder it was to believe in any trap. The smell
of fresh baking was intoxicating.

The monkeys'
mouths began to water and their bellies rumbled.

"I'll take a closer look," volunteered Snout, and ran
off to the cake-laden stand. He broke off a small piece
of cake and slipped it tentatively into his
mouth. It melted on his tongue.

"Heaven," he murmured. Looking up into the trees
he saw dozens of pairs of dazzling shoes sparkling like stars.

"Ah, how beautiful," he gasped. He reached up with his
long arms and unhooked a pair of gold twinkly platform
shoes from a branch. Snout had completely forgotten about
the possible danger and the others waiting for him.

At the edge of the orchard, Wit, Peeper, Peck, Lugs,
Gob, Nit and Bruno were bickering.

"So what if it's a trap? It doesn't matter – no trap can
hold us for long!" said Gob, arrogantly.

"I'm worried, Snout hasn't come back!" said Nit.

"Snout's probably stuffing his face with cake
and leaving none for us," said Bruno.

At these words the monkeys threw caution to
the wind. They found Snout parading around the orchard
in golden shoes eating a big piece of pie. A mad scramble
ensued as they fought for the most beautiful shoes
and stuffed handfuls of cake into their mouths.

The monkeys ate all the delicacies, every single crumb. What a sight they were, faces covered with icing and tummies bloated with cake as they staggered around trying on glittery shoes. They were soon feeling so tired and full that, one by one, they lay down and fell fast asleep.

The guards now crept up very quietly and pounced. The monkeys awoke in a panic. They'd no chance of escape. They were too full and heavy with rich food and couldn't run in their high-heeled shoes. It took no time at all for the guards to catch all of them in their nets. The King had the monkeys placed in his private zoo, but as soon as they came back to their senses they worked out how to escape.

From that day on they stayed in their forest home. Wit spoke for them all when he said: "We've plenty of food in the forest and no need of silly high-heels. Let's stay happy and safe just where we are."

We can all be tempted by greed to do things that are silly and even dangerous. As long as we're safe and well, there's no reason to take more than we actually need.

Angelica and King Frederick

R elax, close your eyes and imagine yourself in an enormous castle. Its thick, stone walls and impressive high towers are surrounded by a great moat. This was the home of King Frederick and Queen Veronica, who were both so busy looking after their kingdom that they didn't have much time for their five children. King Frederick even called his children by numbers rather than by their names because he said it was quicker that way. The royal children were the naughtiest in the land, but one day everything changed. Would you like to know what happened? Listen carefully to their story.

One day the king's children had been even naughtier than usual. They'd teased the royal hunting dogs and dressed up in the chief judge's finest robes. King Frederick was so angry he ordered his guards to keep the children in their bedrooms as punishment. That night he and the queen left the castle for a magnificent ball at a neighbouring duke's palace.

The children waited until their guards had fallen asleep. Then they ran through the castle looking for mischief. At last they reached the picture gallery, which held the portraits of all their royal ancestors. The king was very proud of the gallery and especially loved his own portrait. The queen had ordered the gallery to be repainted and there were lots of paint tins lying around on the floor.

"Who feels like painting?" asked Number 1, the king's eldest daughter, picking up a can of red paint.

She climbed onto a chair, reached up, and painted a red beard and moustache onto her father's portrait. The other children fell about laughing.

"Me next!" cried Number 3.

The children screamed with delight as each tried to outdo the other in painting silly hairstyles and faces on the portraits. Next, they had a paint fight and the whole gallery was spattered in bright colours. Finally they grew tired. Deciding it was time for bed, they crept back to their room.

The king and queen returned from the ball after midnight.

"My dear," said King Frederick to the queen, "I'll take a quick look at the picture gallery. I do like to see the family all together there on the wall. It helps me sleep soundly."

When the king saw the state of the gallery he shouted with fury. "Guards! Who's done this?"

The guards knew the royal children were probably to blame. But they also knew they would be in trouble for failing to keep the children in their rooms.

"It must have been village children, your Majesty," lied the chief guard. "You can see a child's hand prints on the walls."

"Bring all the village children here!" ordered King Frederick. "I don't care if it's the middle of the night."

Soon the picture gallery was full of sleepy children and their worried parents.

"Who did this?" King Frederick demanded, pointing around him at the terrible mess. Nobody said a word.

"If no-one owns up I will punish all the children," he threatened, but still no-one moved.

King Frederick was furious that nobody had confessed. "Guards, lock up all the children!" he cried.

The guards looked guiltily at each other but they were too frightened to say anything. They started separating the village children from their parents.

A small girl called Angelica left her mother's side. She lightly pulled on the king's robe to get his attention.

"Your Majesty," she said, smiling up at his angry red face, "is it fair that the innocent children have to be punished for the actions of a few guilty ones?"

"What?" cried King Frederick. He wasn't used to his orders being questioned. The room fell silent.

"I don't want you to be known as a cruel and unjust king," said Angelica gently.

"If the guilty children won't own up, then all the children must be punished," said King Frederick firmly.

"Does that include your own children?" asked Angelica.

"Of course not, only the village children," replied the king.

"Surely 'all children' must mean *all* children," said the girl.

"The child's right," shouted one of the parents.

"The king's unfair," shouted another.

The king was worried. He looked at Angelica.

"What should I do, child?" he asked.

Angelica thought for a moment. Then she said, "Please bring all the children who live in the castle here."

All the castle's children, including the royal children, were lined up in a row. Angelica looked carefully at them.

"I'm sorry to inform you, your Majesty," she said, "that it's your own family who are guilty."

"You accuse my children!" cried the king.

"Numbers 1, 2, 3, 4 and 5, come here!"

The royal children looked sweet in their white pyjamas, but Angelica asked to see the palms of their hands. The hands of Numbers 1, 2, 3 and 4 were all scrubbed clean. But Number 5, the youngest boy, hadn't removed all the paint from his nails and there was blue paint in his hair.

"My own children, how could you behave in such a way?" cried the king. He turned to Angelica and shook her by the hand. "You've saved me from making a fool of myself. Thank you. But how did you know who was responsible?"

"I didn't at first," said Angelica, "but I did know it couldn't have been the village children. You see, the castle walls are so high and so thick and no-one can swim across the moat."

The king nodded thoughtfully. Then he asked Angelica, "How do you think I should punish my children?"

"Instead of punishing them, spend time with them." said Angelica. "They wouldn't be so naughty if they had more attention from you. And why not call them by their names? Nobody likes to be called a number."

King Frederick shook his head in amazement. He said, "You are an extraordinary and surprising little girl."

Angelica just smiled.

Sometimes situations can seem complicated or unfair. However great the problem, the best solution is always the one that brings a benefit to everybody involved.

The Beautiful White Horse

Relax, close your eyes and picture yourself in the middle of lush grassland. This is the home of a herd of wild horses that roamed free across the plains. Our tale is about one of these horses, a beautiful young filly called Dawn. Dawn's coat was the colour of snow and was so pure and bright that she could even be seen at night. Word spread quickly about this magnificent horse and even reached the ears of the king himself. Would you like to know what happened? Listen carefully to her story.

"I want you to capture this white horse and bring it to me," King Claude said to his guards. "It's only fitting that a handsome man like me should own such a beautiful filly."

It was an easy ride from the palace to the plains and the guards soon spied Dawn drinking her fill at the edge of a lake. They galloped toward her and threw a rope around her neck. The more Dawn struggled, the tighter the rope grew. At last she knew she was caught and the guards led her back to the palace.

The king's courtiers crowded around Dawn, pushing and pulling to get a good look at her. Her neck was sore from the bite of the rope and the terrified creature shook from her mane to her hooves. The king shooed the courtiers aside and stood in front of Dawn.

"You belong to me now. I'm your king and master," he said in a loud, harsh voice that hurt Dawn's ears. She longed to be back running free on the plains where the only sounds were the wind in the grass and the call of birds.

Dawn was shut up in a pen in the stable block. Boris, the stable boy, was a bully. He took great delight in frightening Dawn and prodded her with a broom handle, just for fun.

"I'm in charge of you now, so you'd better behave," Boris warned Dawn. He yanked the rope around her neck hard to make his point.

The king wanted to ride his beautiful white horse through the streets of his city so he could show her off to his people.

"You must train this horse so that she's safe for me to ride," he said to Boris. "If you do a good job I shall reward you with a gold coin."

Boris was greedy and straightaway set about training Dawn. He tried to put a saddle on her back, but she reared up on her hind legs and neighed in fear. The more Boris approached Dawn, the more scared and desperate she grew.

Boris was losing his temper. He picked up a broom and ran toward the horse, as if to strike her. In a wild frenzy Dawn reared up, then dashed as fast she could across the yard. She leapt over the gate and kept on galloping and didn't stop, even when she reached a great forest. Still frightened, she pushed on hard through the trees and bushes.

Dawn was safe now. She was deep in the forest where there were no buildings or roads or paths of any kind and she couldn't be found by the king or his guards. But Dawn did not feel safe. She jumped in fear every time the wind rustled through the leaves or a twig snapped under her hoof – she thought the king's guards had come for her.

A wise old squirrel called Sam sat high in a tree nibbling nuts. He watched the frightened horse paw the ground, twitch her ears and roll her eyes at the slightest sound. It made him sad to see how nervous and upset she was.

"I must help her," said Sam to himself and he climbed down a branch towards Dawn.

"Hello," said Sam, as gently as he could, as Dawn shook her head in terror. "I don't mean to startle you. I only want to talk to you."

Dawn was calmed by Sam's kind voice. She told the old squirrel all that had happened to her.

"I'm very sorry about what happened," said Sam, smiling gently at Dawn. "I can understand how frightened you must have been. The king and his men treated you cruelly. But that's all in the past now. You're safe here and there's no-one who can harm you."

Dawn stopped pawing the ground and listened carefully.

"There's nothing to be frightened of here in the forest," Sam went on. "No humans ever come here. They can't make their way through the thorny bushes and tangled trees. There are only us animals – mice and snails and squirrels and birds – and we're all rather shy ourselves."

Dawn's eyes had stopped rolling now.

"Look around, there's nothing to fear," repeated Sam. "It's just your mind, your own imagination that's frightening you. You're seeing things that are not there. Only your thoughts can scare you here. You just need to control your imagination and you can control your fear," said Sam.

Dawn slowly nodded her head and thought about the squirrel's kind and wise words. She looked around her and saw the trees of the forest and some friendly animals who smiled and winked at her. The king and his guards were a very long way away. She remembered how difficult it had been to make her way this deep into the forest. It would be harder still for humans.

72

Dawn knew Sam was right and she thanked him for his help. And she decided to follow his advice. From now on, she wouldn't let her imagination get the better of her.

Several days passed. Although Dawn was still nervous at times, gradually she became less afraid. When a noise startled her, she calmed herself by thinking through all the possible explanations.

"That's just the trees swaying in the wind," she told herself. Or, "That's just a twig cracking. It's probably Sam coming to visit me, or one of my other new friends."

Dawn used the power of her own mind to control her thoughts. Now she was no longer led by her fear. Little by little she became happy once more and started to enjoy her new, peaceful life in the forest with her caring new friends.

And there was one friend whom she cherished above all – Sam, the wise squirrel, who'd taught her so much.

Sometimes we're so afraid of something that our fear takes over. Remember that you only need to control your imagination and you can control your fear.

Danan and the Serpent

Relax, close your eyes and imagine that you're walking through a dense jungle on a hot and humid day. This tale is about three children, called Keisho, Charini and Danan, whose forest adventure ended up being bigger than they had bargained for. Listen carefully to their story.

"Please can we go on a picnic!" pleaded the children.

"The forest can be a dangerous place," their mother said. "You must all take care. Keisho, you're the eldest and you must look after your sister and brother."

The delighted children set off through the forest. It was very hot and soon their clothes and hair were wet with sweat. They came to a rocky outcrop that cast a deliciously cool shadow and decided to rest there.

"You two set out the picnic, and I'll go to the pond we passed and get some fresh water," said Keisho.

But when he reached the pond, Keisho completely forgot about fetching drinking water. The pond sparkled and glistened and looked very inviting.

"I'll just go for a quick swim," he said to himself. He took off his shirt and waded in.

Suddenly the water began to churn and froth. Keisho gasped in fear as a great serpent rose up from the depths. The serpent's skin was slimy with weeds and its red eyes glared. "Mmm, do I smell lunch?" it hissed.

"Please great serpent, don't eat me," cried Keisho.

"Maybe I will, and maybe I won't," teased the serpent. "If you can answer my question I'll let you go." He smiled at Keisho with all his yellow fangs.

Keisho gulped and nodded. "I'll try."

"Tell me this," hissed the serpent. "What's the wisest thing you've ever learned?"

Keisho frowned with concentration. Then he remembered the advice of his school teachers.

"The way to happiness is to study hard and get a good job," he said.

"Wrong!" cried the serpent. He wrapped himself around Keisho and dragged him deep under water and through a dark tunnel. Just as Keisho thought his lungs would explode, they burst through the water and into a cave. High up on the cave wall was a small hole that let in sunlight and fresh air. Keisho found that he could breathe.

"Welcome to my larder," hissed the serpent. "I'll keep you nice and dry here until I'm ready to eat you."

Charini and Danan were wondering where Keisho was.

"You know what he's like. He probably got distracted," said Charini. She didn't want to frighten her little brother. "You wait here and I'll go and see what's keeping him."

But when Charini reached the pond, she forgot all about Keisho. All she had eyes for was the beautiful blue water glittering in the sunlight. "Oh, I'm so hot. I'll just wade in for a moment to cool down," she said to herself.

As soon as her feet entered the water, the serpent rose from the depths. Charini screamed in fright.

"Mmm, I've got my lunch waiting in my larder, but is this my dinner I smell?" The serpent flicked out his long tongue.

"What have you done with my brother?" cried Charini.

"That's for me to know and for you to find out," said the serpent. "Now, answer me this question and I'll let you go. I might even tell you where your brother is as well."

Charini nodded silently.

"Tell me this," said the serpent. "What's the wisest thing you've ever learned?"

Charini thought about the advice her teachers had given her. "Good little girls should be seen and not heard if they want to be happy," she said.

"Wrong!" cried the serpent. He dragged Charini beneath the water and locked her in the larder with Keisho.

When Charini didn't return, Danan set off to look for his sister and brother. Beside the pond, he saw two sets of footprints going into the water – but none coming out.

The serpent was watching the little boy and saw that Danan stopped at the pond's edge and did not enter the water. "Let's see how clever this young one really is," the serpent thought. He used his powerful magic to give himself the appearance of a woodcutter, then came up to Danan.

"Young friend," the serpent in disguise said, "you look hot and tired. Why not refresh yourself in the cool water?"

Danan always trusted his instincts and something about the woodcutter was not right. "Who are you and what have you done with my brother and sister?" Danan shouted.

The serpent laughed and dropped his disguise. He slithered back into the water. "They waded into my pond. I asked them a simple question that they couldn't answer, so now they are mine. Would you like to try to answer it?"

"If I get the answer right will you set them free?" asked Danan.

"Very well," said the serpent. "Tell me: what's the wisest thing you've ever learned?"

Danan thought for some time.

"Well?" said the serpent.

"I don't have all day. I have lunch to prepare."

78

Danan couldn't think at all when he was anxious. So he took a deep breath and did his best to relax. He recalled sitting on his father's knee as a very young child. What was it his father had said? Then he remembered.

"Don't harm yourself or others and be kind to everyone; then you'll have a good life," said Danan.

"Well done," said the serpent. "You've shown great wisdom. I'll release your brother and sister." He dived into the pond and brought Keisho and Charini to the surface.

The serpent called out, "To be truly wise, you must put into practice these wise words; otherwise they are meaningless." With this he disappeared.

The three children hugged each other in great relief. From that day on they did their best to be kind to everyone they met. And whenever they were tempted to wade into a pond again, they always checked carefully for serpents first.

Living a worthwhile life means doing our best at all times and showing goodwill toward others. This also means not doing things that harm ourselves and others.

The Spirit of the Tree

Relax, close your eyes and picture yourself riding a camel across a vast desert under a scorching sun. This tale is about a camel breeder called Big Tam and his son Goza. They were bringing a herd of camels to market when something very strange happened. Would you like to know what it was? Listen carefully to their story.

After travelling for many days, Big Tam and Goza reached the walls of the great city called Miraz. Outside the city gates grew an ancient tree with branches crooked like witches' fingers. People said that the tree had been there longer than the city, protected by a powerful spirit. As the camel train passed by, Big Tam knelt before the old tree.

"Oh wondrous tree spirit, please help me make lots of money selling camels today at the market. I promise a great offering to you in return," said Big Tam. He walked round the tree three times, bowing and clapping.

"What are you doing, Dad?" asked Goza. He thought his father's behaviour was a bit odd.

"I'm asking the tree spirit to bless us with good luck at the market today," said Big Tam.

"My school teacher says that asking spirits for help is silly. She says you make your own luck," said Goza.

They passed through the city gates. Secretly, Big Tam rubbed the lucky coin he kept in his pocket and whispered, "Help us, little coin." He made sure his son didn't see.

The market square bustled with people from many lands, the stalls piled high with fruit and vegetables, jewelry, pottery and carpets. Big Tam set to work, haggling with the camel buyers. By late afternoon all his camels had been sold.

"Our luck was in, my boy," said Big Tam, grinning. "Now let's go home." But, as they left the city, he stopped to buy two goats. When they reached the old tree, he knelt down, grasping the goats, and pulled a knife from his belt.

"What are you going to do, Dad?" Goza cried out in fear.

"I'm going to sacrifice these goats to the tree spirit. I'm giving thanks for our good luck today at the market."

"Oh no, don't do that!" cried Goza. "Don't hurt them!" As he spoke something incredible happened. Rain fell from the branches and turned to mist, and from the mist floated the figure of a woman. Her hair streamed around her and her robes sparkled like diamonds.

Big Tam dropped his knife. "Who are you?" he gasped.

"I'm the spirit of this tree. That wasn't rain, but my tears for these poor frightened animals. Your good luck, as you call it, at the market today was only due to your own hard work. You should listen to your son!"

Big Tam was beginning to feel rather silly kneeling before the tree spirit. He stood up awkwardly and blushed.

"Spirits nurture all that lives," she continued. "We don't waste our time helping humans bargain at the market." She smiled before disappearing back into the tree.

Big Tam and Goza stood staring at the spot where she had floated. "Here's a present for you," declared Big Tam at last, giving his 'lucky' coin to Goza. "Buy something special with it. I won't be needing it any longer."

From that day on, Big Tam and Goza worked hard together to make their own good fortune.

It's through our own efforts that we make our own good luck and find happiness. Trying to make things happen through relying on luck or the power of others will get us nowhere.

Egbert and the Fisherman

Relax, close your eyes and imagine a duke's son, Egbert, who thought he was the most important person in the world. Egbert believed he could be as rude as he liked and order everyone about – until a kindly fisherman taught him an important lesson. Listen carefully to his story.

One morning Egbert was being carried around the palace in a sedan chair by his servants, Benson and Merriweather. It wasn't that Egbert couldn't walk – he was very lazy and didn't like to do anything for himself.

"I want to go boating," Egbert said to Benson.

"But Master Egbert, there's a storm coming!" stuttered Benson. He was scared – he knew Egbert didn't like it when people said no to him.

"I don't care, I'm the duke's son and I want to go boating right NOW!" shouted Egbert.

Benson and Merriweather, puffing and panting, carried Egbert and his sedan chair down the one hundred and eight steps of the palace, out of the gate and toward the sea.

"Watch it, you're bumping me," complained Egbert.

The two exhausted servants hauled Egbert along the rocky road to the harbour. Egbert moaned and groaned, then demanded to be carried faster. Merriweather finally lost his temper. He gave the sedan chair an almighty push and Benson dropped it, too. "I've had enough of you and your wicked tongue!" Merriweather cried.

Egbert and the chair rolled down the hill, out of control. Sorry that he'd lost his temper, Merriweather ran with Benson after Egbert, but they couldn't stop him plopping into the sea with a great splash. Clinging to the chair, Egbert bobbed up and down in the water.

Just then the storm arrived. Lightning flashed across the sky and the waves were whipped high by the wind. Egbert had never been so frightened.

"Help!" he cried. "Please somebody, help me!"

Ayo was a fisherman who'd also been caught by the storm. But he was very experienced and very calm. He'd hauled in his sail and was patiently waiting for the storm to pass. He spun his ship hard in the direction of Egbert's cries.

Another flash of lightning lit up Egbert clinging to his sedan chair in the sea. Ayo thought quickly. "I'll haul him in with my fishing net," he said to the pet parrot who kept him company. Ayo threw out his net, caught Egbert first time and pulled him aboard.

Egbert lay on the deck, feeling very sorry for himself.
"You're a strange-looking fish!" chuckled Ayo.

"How disrespectful. I'm a duke's son! How dare he laugh,"
thought Egbert furiously. But he said nothing. He was
frightened of this man with his tattoos and eye-patch.

"Come on," said Ayo, ruffling Egbert's hair "We'll get
you dried off and get some warm soup in you."

Egbert was red-hot with anger. "How dare he touch
me with his great peasant hands," he thought.

The storm passed and Ayo sailed safely into port.
Egbert pretended to be grateful. He tried to smile, but it
hurt his face as he wasn't used to smiling. He said "thank
you," but felt sick speaking that unfamiliar word out loud.

To Ayo's face he said: "When I'm made duke I will
reward you most generously." But under his breath Egbert
added "As if ...!"

When Egbert returned to the palace he bragged that
he had saved himself using his brainpower and his excellent
swimming. But everyone knew that Egbert never bothered
to use his brain, and what's more never did any exercise.
"He doesn't even walk anywhere, let alone swim," they said.

The following year Ayo was sailing near the duke's
harbour. "Perhaps I'll pay a visit to my young friend," Ayo
said to his parrot. "Let's see how he's getting along."

Egbert's father had died and Egbert was now the duke. The morning that Ayo decided to visit, Egbert was lying under a big red canopy on the palace terrace having his toes massaged. He spied the great hulk of Ayo coming up the hill.

"Aha, that disrespectful oaf is back, looking for handouts," he thought. "I must get rid of him before he tells anyone he rescued me." Egbert shouted to his guards: "Arrest that man! He's a thief and a thug. Throw him in the dungeon."

Egbert's bodyguards didn't dare challenge him. They arrested Ayo, bound his hands and took him to the dungeon.

It was market day in the city square. Traders were selling fruit and vegetables, spices and fresh fish. Paolo the grocer spied his friend Ayo being led away in chains and demanded to know where the guards were taking him.

"He is being sent to the dungeons. He's a thug and a thief," replied the chief guard.

"Nonsense," exclaimed Paolo. "I know this man and he's a decent and honest fellow."

A crowd gathered and several others recognized Ayo.

Mario the spice trader said: "He's the kindest man I know."

Nino the goldsmith said: "Ayo helps everyone he can."

And Claude the fishmonger said: "I'd trust Ayo with my life. What's more, I know that Ayo saved Duke Egbert's life." Then Claude told the gathering crowd the whole story.

"Egbert is ungrateful and a liar," the people cried. The angry crowd ran to the palace demanding justice.

"Down with Egbert! Ayo for chief minister!" they cried. Ashamed and frightened, Egbert didn't know what to do.

"Let Ayo decide on Egbert's punishment," said Paolo.

Ayo thought for a while. Then he said, "Egbert should be a fisherman for one year and one day. I can't think of a better way of teaching him patience and humility."

After a year and a day as a poor fisherman, Egbert had learned the value of helping people and was grateful when people helped him in turn. He became kind and generous and relied on Ayo as his wise counsellor. The people of the dukedom agreed they had the best ruler in the land.

However important we are, we all need the help of other people. Using kind and generous words is the best way of making sure we receive support and friendship from others.

Amrita and
the Elephants

Relax, close your eyes and picture a little Indian girl called Amrita who was always worrying. One day she worried so much she managed to frighten not just herself but her entire village. Would you like to know what happened? Listen carefully to her story.

It was a lovely sunny afternoon and Amrita was sitting under a tree at the edge of the forest. Birds twittered in the branches and fluffy white clouds sailed across the sky.

"I don't like the look of those clouds," Amrita was thinking to herself. "It's sunny now, but what if it starts to rain? I'll be completely soaked by the time I get home."

Amrita began to wring her hands. "And what if it rains and rains and there's a flood? Everything will be washed away – the farms, the animals and the village, too!"

Just at that moment the ground began to shake, there was an almighty crash, and a wave of dust rolled through the trees toward her. Birds flew from the branches into the sky, squawking in alarm.

"What could that be?" Amrita cried out. "It must be an earthquake! Nothing else could make that much noise!" She scrambled to her feet in terror.

"I must run away," she told herself. "I must run for my life!"

Amrita didn't wait to see what was happening in the forest. If she had, she would have seen a group of young elephants playing chase among the trees. Even though they were only young, the elephants were still very large and very heavy – and the ground shook beneath their feet.

Amrita ran away from the trees and up to the village. She ran right past her two friends Tylanni and Gomin, who were racing their bikes along the street.

"What's wrong, Amrita?" they called out.

"The world's ending," cried Amrita, who kept on running.

"What do you mean, the world's ending?" asked Tylanni, frightened already. She and Gomin chased after Amrita.

"There was a great earthquake! I saw trees crashing to the ground! Our village will be destroyed!" cried Amrita.

The children shrieked. As they hurried through the village, everyone they met grew afraid as well.

"What's wrong?" people asked. "What's happened?"

"It's the end of the world," Amrita called out breathlessly.

Word spread through the village that the world was ending. A crowd of frightened children and adults were soon running in panic, looking for somewhere to hide. The donkeys, horses, cows, pigs, cats and dogs were all running, too. Everyone was following Amrita.

Ashoka, Amrita's father, saw his daughter charging up the hill toward their house, followed by a huge crowd.

He put his hands up and shouted very loudly, "Stop!"

"Daddy, the world's ending!" cried Amrita.

"It's an earthquake," shouted Eila, the mechanic.

"No, I heard it was a tornado," yelled Akash, the postman.

"You're both wrong, the moon is falling out of the sky," cried Deepa, the baker.

Donkeys brayed, dogs barked, cats meowed and pigs squealed. The crowd stopped running and fell into arguing about how the world was ending.

Ashoka lifted his daughter up into his arms. She felt safe there and began to calm down. Ashoka asked the crowd, "Why are you so frightened?"

"There was an earthquake," answered Rahul, the farmer.

"Who felt the earthquake?" asked Ashoka.

"My friend Chiko told me," said Rahul.

"I was told by Gomin and Tylanni," said Chiko.

"Gomin and Tylanni, what did you see?" asked Ashoka.

"Oh, we didn't see anything, Amrita told us about it," they explained.

"It's true Daddy, I felt the earthquake," said Amrita.

"Tell me what happened," said Ashoka.

"Well, I was sitting under a tree at the edge of the forest, when the earth began to shake and tremble. I heard trees crash behind me, and a huge wave of dust rolled over me. There were screams and screeches from the animals. It was awful and really frightening." As Amrita spoke, her voice began to quiver with fear again.

"All right, I think we should go and have a look in the forest," said Ashoka.

"Oh no, Daddy, I'm too scared. We'll be killed. We should get as far away as possible," cried Amrita.

"You'll be fine. I'll keep you safe. You know I wouldn't let anything happen to you," said Ashoka gently to his daughter.

Ashoka carried Amrita back to the forest. The crowd followed cautiously at a distance.

As they got close Amrita cried out. "See, Daddy, the trees have fallen down! And listen to the animals!" She covered her eyes with her hands.

"Amrita, it's okay. The world's not ending," said her father.

When Amrita opened her eyes she saw the young elephants chasing each other through the trees, trumpeting in excitement. As they crashed into the trees, the earth shook and clouds of dust rose from beneath their huge feet.

Ashoka turned to his daughter. "You frightened yourself," he said. "The elephants are just playing.

There was nothing to be afraid of, provided you didn't get too close to them. Next time you feel frightened, take time to check what's actually happening. Don't rush to act before you have enough information."

Amrita nodded her head slowly.

"You see, my daughter, how you have needlessly frightened yourself and the whole village? And this all happened through the power of your mind."

Amrita bowed her head. "I'm sorry Daddy. I'll try not to jump to conclusions in future."

Ashoka hugged his daughter. "All right then, let's go home now." They turned and walked toward the village.

"So the world's not ending?" asked a latecomer as the crowd drifted away and people went back to their work.

"No, not today," laughed Amrita. "I made a mistake. It was all in my imagination."

The mind is very powerful and jumping to conclusions can get you into all sorts of bother. Take time to be sure of what you have actually seen, heard or felt before deciding what to do next.

The Lion
and the Boar

Relax, close your eyes, and picture yourself living deep in a jungle. This tale is about a rude boar called Benny, whose bragging got him into serious trouble. Would you like to know what happened? Listen carefully to his story.

One morning Benny and some deer were taking a drink at a waterhole. As usual, Benny was talking about himself. "I lost my tusk in a fight with a ferocious tiger!" he said loudly.

The deer ignored him. Everyone agreed that Benny the Boar was a real bore! He was also a liar. They knew he'd caught his tusk on tree roots while foraging for mushrooms.

But Benny went on boasting: "See this scar on my hind leg? That's from when I taught a crocodile a lesson!"

Just then a huge lion emerged from the trees. All the animals fell silent, even Benny. All you could hear was the "sip, sip" of the thirsty lion, whose name was Rory. He finished his drink, wished the animals good morning and left.

Once Benny was sure the lion had gone he started to laugh loudly. "Ha! That silly lion was scared away by me!"

"Ssh! He'll hear you," said the deer. "Your foolish tongue is going to get you in trouble one of these days!"

"I'm the real king of the jungle!" gloated Benny. Come and fight, you big, ugly scaredy-cat!"

Rory burst through the trees. His teeth were bared, his mane stood up on end and his tail twitched angrily. "You need a lesson in manners, you impudent boar!"

The deer scattered. Benny shook from snout to hoof.

"If I hadn't had a big lunch I would sort you out right now. We'll meet here tomorrow instead!" snarled Rory.

Rory disappeared and Benny slumped onto the ground. "What am I to do?" he wailed. He was very frightened. After much fruitless worrying, he fell asleep.

Next morning, a skunk called Peewee, mistaking Benny for a rock, climbed onto his head for some sunbathing. Benny woke with a start and wailed again: "Oh, what am I to do?"

Peewee fell startled to the ground. "A talking rock!" he laughed. "Excuse me, Mr Boar. Now, what's the matter?"

Relieved to hear a kind voice, Benny told Peewee how he'd been rude to the lion. He also confessed all the lies he'd ever told. I thought everyone would like me if I sounded important," said Benny sadly. "But that didn't seem to work."

"You shouldn't be rude to anyone, especially not a polite, noble lion like Rory," said Peewee. "Now, I have an idea.

It's not a pleasant one, but it might sort out your problem."

"I'll do anything," cried Benny.

"Sshh, calm down," said Peewee. "I'll give you a spray of skunk perfume." He lifted his tail and sprayed Benny.

"Ugh!" cried Benny. "I stink!"

Just then Rory appeared. "EEEooww! What's that terrible smell?" He covered his nose with his paws.

"It's me. But can I say first I'm very sorry I was so rude," said Benny, sincerely. "From now on if I haven't got anything nice to say, I won't say anything at all."

Rory looked at Benny. At last he said, "I'll not fight you today or any day. I couldn't do anything worse to you than you've done to yourself." He chuckled and left.

A relieved Benny jumped into the watering hole.

That night as the sun set, the two new friends, Benny and Peewee, kindly wished each other a good night's sleep.

Boasting or being rude to people won't impress them or gain you any friends in the long run. Kind and thoughtful words are best, for your own benefit as well as for that of other people.

Tim and Grandpa Joe

Relax, close your eyes and imagine that you're in the countryside, surrounded by rolling green hills and flower-filled meadows. This is where Tim lived. His grandpa, Joe, was a mailman and one day, when the mail van broke down, Grandpa Joe asked Tim if he could help him with the deliveries. And delivering the mail turned out to be full of adventure. Would you like to know what happened? Listen carefully to their story.

The sun was rising as Grandpa Joe and a yawning young Tim set off on the morning mail round. Tim struggled a little under the weight of the mailbags. But he didn't complain. Grandpa Joe was so pleased to have his help.

"With the van at the garage, I couldn't manage these bags all by myself," said Grandpa Joe. "I'm getting older now, you know. And it will be nice to have your company, too. But tell me if the bags get too heavy, Tim."

As the sun climbed higher into the sky, Grandpa Joe and Tim walked together along the winding country roads.

After a while Tim started to feel tired and the mailbags seemed to get heavier with every step. He tried to distract himself from his discomfort by whistling. He didn't want to let Grandpa Joe know he was struggling.

Just then they turned a bend and came upon a lamb caught in a prickly hedge. The lamb was very distressed and bleating in pain. Tim forgot all about his arms aching with the weight of the mailbags. He put the bags down and ran to the hedge as fast as he could, then he and Grandpa Joe worked to free the frightened lamb. The thorns scratched Tim's arms and hands, but at last the lamb was free.

"We'd better try to find this lamb's mother," said Grandpa Joe.

"There are sheep in the next field," said Tim excitedly as he looked over the fence. "Perhaps the mother isn't far away."

Gently holding the lamb, Tim climbed over the fence. He ran across the field to a stile and climbed into the next field. A sheep came up to him, bleating loudly. Tim put the lamb down and it skipped up to the sheep and nestled in close.

"That must be his mother," called Grandpa Joe, smiling.

Tim rejoined Grandpa Joe in the road and they continued on their way.

"We helped that lamb, Grandpa," said Tim.

"You did most of the hard work," said Grandpa Joe and he patted Tim on the back. "Well done."

"The strangest thing is I don't feel tired and my arms aren't aching anymore," Tim said to himself. He thought about how good it was to help others.

"When I grow up I'm going to help animals or people," he promised himself. "I could be a vet or a doctor."

The morning grew warmer. After a while, Tim began to feel the weight of the mailbags and the pain in his arms again. He began to feel sorry for himself and wished he had never agreed to help Grandpa Joe.

"I should have stayed at home. I could still be in bed or playing in the garden," Tim thought.

The darker Tim's thoughts grew, the heavier his load felt. All he could think about was getting rid of the bags he was carrying. Tim even started to feel angry with Grandpa Joe for asking him to help with the deliveries. Tim was so caught up in his black thoughts that he didn't notice Grandpa Joe had led him off the road toward a farmhouse.

"Listen, Tim," said Grandpa Joe. "Someone's crying."

They found the farmer's wife, Mrs Brown, sitting in the middle of the farmyard, sobbing. Tim forgot his angry thoughts and together he and Grandpa Joe hurried over to find out what was wrong.

"I tripped and sprained my ankle. I can't get up, and the poor animals haven't been fed," cried Mrs Brown.

"Don't worry," said Grandpa Joe. "We'll help you."

In no time at all Grandpa Joe had got Mrs Brown up and helped her hobble back to the farmhouse. He sat her down in a chair and lifted her sprained ankle onto a footstool.

"That'll help reduce the swelling," he said.

Tim took care of all the animals. He scattered seed for the chickens that were scratching about in the yard, he gave the pigs food scraps from the kitchen, and he put fresh hay in the stables for the horses and the cows.

"You've done so much for me," said Mrs Brown. She pointed at a tray of chocolate muffins. "Please take some of those as a thank you. I baked them this morning."

Tim felt contented after helping Mrs Brown, just as he had after rescuing the lamb. He found that he had lots of energy and was no longer tired. "Perhaps I will become a teacher or a fireman when I grow up," he said to himself. "Helping people really is wonderful."

Grandpa Joe and Tim continued on their way. The hot sun blazed down and the dust on the road made Tim cough. He began to forget his happy thoughts again. He looked at the road stretching endlessly in front and thought to himself, "No-one is helping me. I've helped all these people today but what have I got in return? I should just look after myself."

Tim's bags felt bigger and heavier than ever and his anger caused an ache in his heart.

But then he remembered Mrs Brown and the lamb. And he remembered how pleased his grandfather had been when he'd agreed to help him on the mail round. Every time he had helped people he'd felt warm and happy and the mailbags had seemed easier to carry. 'People have been helping me all day,' thought Tim.

He realized all he needed now was a rest and then he would be able to carry on. Nothing else was wrong.

"Grandpa Joe, I'm sorry but I'm feeling really tired. Could we sit down and have a rest?" asked Tim.

"Of course, Tim," said Grandpa Joe. "It's important to know when to stop. You've done really well today. It's not easy to carry these heavy bags such a long way."

They sat down and Grandpa Joe pulled out a flask of tea and they each ate one of Mrs Brown's muffins. And the muffin was the most delicious Tim had ever tasted.

It's easy to blow problems out of proportion when we only focus on our feelings. When we take care of others, as well as ourselves, everyone benefits and problems become opportunities.

The Desert Willow

Relax, close your eyes and picture yourself standing in front of the most beautiful tree you have ever seen. It has graceful branches and long slender leaves and it's covered in pink flowers. The tree stands alone in a vast, parched desert. It's called the Desert Willow and it's home to two parrots, a colony of ants, a hive of bees and several hairy spiders. All the animals love the shade and protection of the willow and they all lived happily together until, one day, some unwelcome guests arrived. Would you like to know what happened? Listen carefully to their story.

It was midday. The sun hung shimmering in a cloudless blue sky. Hidden among the leaves of the willow rested the parrots, Priscilla and Percy. They dozed and dreamed of the cooler days to come. The ants and spiders rested, too, but the busy bees continued to work hard, gathering nectar from the lovely pink flowers.

In the distance a sandstorm rolled toward the willow. It blew in one direction across the desert and then another, all the time drawing closer to the tree. Suddenly the sandstorm hit the tree with all its force! The tree shook and woke the parrots from their nap. When the dust settled, three new animals who'd been swept up and carried along in the sandstorm, were at the foot of the tree. There was a snake, a rat and a pig and they were all very angry.

"My snout is sore," complained Pig.

"It's your own fault!" said Snake, sticking out his tongue at Pig. "You said we didn't need to take shelter."

"No, it's Rat's fault," retorted Pig. "He said he could navigate us safely through the sandstorm."

"I can see stars," said Rat, wobbling his head in a daze.

The startled parrots, bees, ants and spiders watched the visitors arguing below them.

After a while Rat, Snake and Pig stopped their bickering.

"I'm starving," said Pig. He began snuffling around the roots of the tree with his snout, looking for food.

"Look around you. We're in the middle of a desert. There's nothing but dirt here!" said Rat.

"Ssh, listen, can you hear buzzing?" hissed Snake.

"Where there's buzzing, there are bees," said Rat.

"And where there are bees, there's sure to be delicious, sweet honey!" said Pig.

The bees stopped their work on hearing these words.

Frightened, they flew quickly to warn their queen, Sophia. "What are we to do?" they asked her.

Sophia was very clever but she couldn't think of any way to save their precious honey. She asked the ants, the parrots and the hairy spiders, but no-one knew what to do.

"We are no match for those large and clever animals," said Thunder, the chief of the ants.

"Let's think, what are our strengths?" asked Sophia.

"We ants are very small but very strong," said Thunder.

"I'm afraid all we can do is spin webs," said the spiders.

"Priscilla and I can mimic any sound we hear," said Percy the parrot, in a voice that sounded very like Queen Sophia's. At this everyone laughed and relaxed a little. Feeling calmer, Queen Sophia could think more clearly. She came up with an excellent idea, which she shared with them all.

Meanwhile Pig, Snake and Rat were making their plans to get the honey. "Snake, you climb onto the back of Pig, then I'll climb up on top of you. From there I can reach a branch and lift myself into the tree," said Rat.

Each animal did as Rat said. As Rat stretched up to reach a branch, he suddenly found that he was swaying.

"Stay still, you silly Pig," hissed Rat.

"Help! The ground is moving!" cried Pig.

Unseen by Pig, the tiny ants had crept underneath him.

With their combined strength they lifted him away from the tree. As Pig scrambled back to solid ground, he, Snake and Rat all came tumbling down. The ants scattered, giggling.

Again, Pig, Snake and Rat tried to balance on each other's backs. Again, the ants crept out from the willow's roots and lifted Pig away. And again, he tumbled down in fright. But the third time Rat, Snake and Pig tried to climb into the tree, the ants were too exhausted to stop them.

Pig clung to his branch nervously. He wasn't good at climbing and moved up very, very slowly.

Just above him, Percy and Priscilla, the parrots, were hiding on a branch. Percy hissed out loud in a voice that sounded like Snake's: "Hey, stupid Pig, get a move on."

"Lazy Pig!" cried Priscilla, sounding just like Rat.

"Who are you calling stupid and lazy?" grunted Pig. As he turned toward the voices, he lost his grip on the branch and fell out of the tree. "Ouch!" he cried.

Snake had climbed high up into the tree when a voice very like Rat's called out: "Quick, quick! Over here!" It was Percy, pretending to be Rat.

Snake slithered off in the direction of the voice and was caught in a large mass of sticky spider webs. He lost his balance and landed on Pig. They both lay dizzy on the ground.

Rat didn't care about Pig or Snake. "There'll be all the more honey for me," he said to himself. He climbed up to the beehive, his nose twitching with the smell of honey. But now Queen Sophia began to sing and as she did so the bees swarmed before the hive. Rat was hypnotized by her buzzing and by the bees' ever-changing patterns.

"I feel so sleepy," Rat yawned out loud. "I can't seem to keep my eyes open." He lost his grip on the branch and fell onto Pig and Snake on the ground below.

The tree began to shake with the buzzing of angry bees. They flew out of the tree in a great swarm toward the dazed trio, who picked themselves up and ran away as fast as they could. The bees chased them until they were sure that Pig, Snake and Rat could never find their way back.

"We may be small but together we're very powerful," said Queen Sophia, and all the animals cheered.

Whoever we are, even if we feel very small and unimportant, we have gifts that we can share with others. And sharing helps not just us, but also our friends and family.

Antonio and His Treasure

Relax, close your eyes and imagine a long table piled high with gold pieces in the great hall of a palace. Counting the coins is the king's treasurer, a man called Antonio. He'd once been a generous man, but people said that counting gold had turned his heart cold and hard. Every night, after he had finished at the palace, Antonio would return to his house and count his own gold. But one day Antonio had a great fright that was to change him for ever. Listen carefully to his story.

It was a cold winter's evening as Antonio walked back to his house. He stopped by an inn and looked through the open window. "I would love a nice hot drink," he thought, "but I mustn't waste good money on such silly things."

As Antonio walked home through the snow, he grew colder and colder and more and more grumpy.

"What's wrong?" asked his wife Rosa when she saw him. "Your face is so long your jaw might hit the ground."

"I really want a hot fruit drink," Antonio replied moodily.

"Oh heavens, is that all?" Rosa exclaimed. "Why don't I make a big jug of hot fruit punch and invite the neighbours around. We can have a little party," she suggested hopefully.

"And who'll be paying for this party?" asked Antonio.

Rosa sighed. "If you're worried about the cost I'll make just enough punch for our household," she said.

"Are you suggesting we spend good money on the servants? That's extravagant," said Antonio.

"All right, I'll make just enough punch for you, me and our children," said Rosa.

Antonio thought for a moment. "The children are too young to appreciate it," he said.

"What if I make just enough for you and me?" asked Rosa. She was getting fed up now.

Antonio's jaw dropped. "Surely you don't want any, do you?" he asked. "I'll send a servant to the inn to buy me a tankard of fruit punch." He carefully took one gold coin from his purse. When the servant returned Antonio grabbed the tankard and went straight upstairs to his bedroom. He climbed into bed and drank all the punch. Then he fell into a troubled sleep, upset about having spent a whole gold coin.

What Antonio didn't know was that Dusty, a house sprite, had been watching all that had taken place. Dusty looked just like a person but he was as small as a mouse. He wore a brown tunic and a brown cap perched on his head.

114

"You're a very greedy man," said Dusty to the sleeping Antonio. "It's time for you to learn about sharing!"

There was a puff of smoke, a sneeze and a hiccup, then the smoke cleared. Dusty the sprite was no longer there. In his place stood a second Antonio!

Dusty picked up Antonio's purse filled with gold coins. "Let's put this money to good use," he said. Then he let himself out of the bedroom and locked Antonio inside.

"Rosa, my turtle dove, where are you?" called Dusty in Antonio's voice. "I'm sorry for being so mean earlier. Let's have a party and invite all the neighbours."

"Oh, Antonio, that would make me so happy," said Rosa, amazed to see her husband smiling cheerfully. "But this is very unlike you. Are you feeling quite well?"

"I've never felt better!" Dusty said with a smile. "I've turned over a new leaf." Then the sprite took out Antonio's purse. "Spend all this money on whatever you need."

Rosa called all her friends and neighbours to the house. When the party was in full swing, Dusty started offering the guests the most expensive ornaments and furniture as gifts.

"May you live to be a hundred, generous Antonio!" cried his neighbour Benita. "May I take this beautiful lamp from your hallway? I've long admired it."

115

"Of course!" said Dusty and Rosa together.

The sound of people laughing, talking and carrying away his goods finally woke Antonio.

"What's all that noise?" he wondered.

From his balcony he saw a crowd of people carrying off his possessions. He was speechless with rage. His neighbour Benita looked up to the balcony and waved. "Thank you for being so generous, just as you always used to be!" she called.

Antonio broke open the locked bedroom door and rushed downstairs.

"Rosa, I am being robbed, help!" he cried.

Rosa appeared with Dusty the sprite by her side. Dusty still looked exactly like Antonio. On one side stood the real Antonio, shaking and angry. In the doorway stood another Antonio, smiling and happy and holding Rosa by the hand.

Rosa looked from one Antonio to the other.

"What's going on?" she asked, completely confused.

"He's an impostor," shouted Antonio. "You're my wife!"

Rosa looked at the shouting, angry Antonio, then she turned back to the smiling, gentle Dusty.

"This is my Antonio, the kind and generous man I married. Throw that horrible imposter into the street."

There was a great puff of smoke.

Once it had cleared, Dusty the sprite appeared in his true, tiny form. Antonio and Rosa couldn't believe their eyes.

"Rosa, I'm not Antonio, I'm Dusty the house sprite. Antonio, when you were young and poor you were a happy man. Now you work only for gold, but gold cannot make you happy. It's only sharing gold that gives it any purpose. Change your ways or you will lose your home and your possessions and, worse still, your wife and children."

Antonio was terrified to think of all that he could lose. "I promise to be kind and generous, as I once was," he said. "I now realize what is truly important. And it isn't gold."

From that day onward Antonio returned to being the man Rosa remembered. He shared his money and his possessions generously. And he realized that he gained great joy from seeing the people he cared for happy. That was worth far more than his gold.

What we choose to do in our lives affects our mind and our heart. Think carefully about the work you would like to do when you grow up. Will it help you to help others?

Preparing to Meditate

Although the practice of meditation is often associated with Eastern philosophy and religion, we are all born with the innate ability to meditate. Even if we don't know it, we all experience its calming effects when we are completely absorbed in a particular activity – for example, while listening to music. At such times, we feel content, peaceful and at one with the world.

It's a good idea to be fully prepared before meditation. Your child should wear warm, loose clothing and should wash his hands and face before beginning in order to cleanse himself symbolically of his everyday activities. Then choose a quiet place where interruptions are unlikely, turn off any phones, and dim any lights. When all the practical preparations have been completed, he can relax and get comfortable.

Begin by teaching your child a relaxation exercise. This is important as it helps your child focus on the here and now, moving out of his thoughts. Lie on the floor alongside your child and ask him to begin by breathing deeply for at least a minute. Count out the in and out breaths, so that there are at least four deep inhales and four deep exhales at a time. Then ask your child to clench and then relax each part of his body in turn. Guide him so that he starts by pointing and then relaxing his feet, lifting and then relaxing each leg, clenching and relaxing each fist, lifting each arm, gently turning the head left and right until the whole body has been relaxed in turn.

Now ask your child to concentrate on each part of his body in turn once more, but this time sending a message of deep relaxation and stillness to every muscle. Ask your child to breathe deeply once more, taking a deep breath through his nostrils, imagining the air coming deep into his skull and then the same breath moving down his spine to his tailbone. Then asking him to imagine the breath returning back up the spine, back through the skull and out through his nostrils again. Continue this exercise (a breathing meditation known as "Shining Skull") guiding your child through the in breath and out breath.

The quality of a meditation session is more important than its length, and the more regularly we practice, the greater the benefits we enjoy. Try to get your child to meditate at the same time in the same place each day. Bedtime is the best for most children as they can go to sleep straight afterward. Naturally, the length of time that they are able to sit for will vary from child to child, but they will soon get an idea of what is appropriate by how it makes them feel.

If you're guiding your child's meditation, speak in a slow, relaxed voice, pausing from time to time to let your words sink in, so that he can conjure up the scene as vividly as possible. It's important to let him know that it's natural for his mind to wander and that, if this happens, all he has to do is bring his attention back to his body.

Beautiful White Horse Meditation

This meditation is inspired by the story of the same name, and can help calm your child when he or she is highly stressed.

Close your eyes and take some deep breaths in and out. Picture yourself in a forest. Enormous trees tower above you and ferns rise up on either side of the path you're walking along. It's very calm and peaceful here. All you can hear is the sound of the rustling leaves and the call of birds.

You're breathing very slowly and deeply now. Sunlight dapples the path and you find that you're trotting gently along it. You look down at your feet and you see that they are hooves. You nod your head and you discover you have a flowing white mane. You realize you're a beautiful white horse.

You're perfectly safe and happy. Through the power of your mind you're able to make yourself calm. You're completely at peace with everything around you, and you feel so calm and relaxed now that you lie down and have a rest in a clearing.

You lie down on the ground and you realize you're no longer a horse but yourself once more. You're calm and relaxed just as you were when you were a horse, you're in control of your mind and you know that your mind is strong and powerful. You get up now and walk back along the path, back to where the forest ends, back home once more, carrying the knowledge of the strength and calmness of your mind with you.

Crossing the River Meditation

This meditation is inspired by the story 'Ester and Lucky', and can help your child discover the rewards of helping others.

Close your eyes and take some deep breaths in and out. Picture yourself walking through a tropical jungle. You look down and see that you have huge grey feet, then you notice something swishing in front of you and realize it's your trunk. You're an enormous and powerful elephant.

You come to a village beside a great river. The river is in flood – it's flowing fast and you can see the remains of a bridge that has been washed away. You see a young woman crying and you ask her what the matter is. She tells you that, because the bridge has washed away, she can't get back to her family.

You tell her not to worry and ask her to climb onto your back, because you can safely carry her across. You slowly wade into the river. You can feel the current pulling against your legs, but you're very strong and brave and carefully and calmly you make your way across the river to the bank on the other side.

Your legs are aching, but the woman hugs you and tells you what a kind elephant you are, and the feeling of great joy this gives you rises up powerfully through your entire body.

You start to walk back along the jungle path home and you are no longer an elephant now, but a child. Your heart is rich remembering the feeling of happiness.

Magic Moonlight Tree Meditation

This meditation is based on the tree featured in the story of the same name. It's also inspired by the Buddhist meditation known as *metta bhavana* or "the development of loving kindness", and will help your child discover the rewards of compassion.

Close your eyes and take some deep breaths in and out. It's nighttime and you're standing beneath the most beautiful tree you have ever seen. Its leaves are a vivid blue and shaped like stars and from its branches hang shiny silver-coloured fruits. You pick one of the fruits from the branches. It smells more delicious than mangoes, peaches or strawberries, and you take another deep breath to inhale its scent once more.

As you gaze up at the tree you can see that brightly coloured pieces of cloth have been tied to the branches and that a message is printed on each piece of cloth. You can't quite reach the pieces of cloth so you climb up a lower branch of the tree until you're sitting safely and comfortably. You carefully untie the piece of cloth and read the message. It says: "May you be well, may you be happy."

You close your eyes and breathe deeply as you think about the message. You sense a deep warmth in your chest like a golden sun, and you can feel its radiance spreading out around you along all the branches of the tree to the very tips of the leaves.

You re-tie the cloth to the tree branch and climb a

little higher up amongst the branches until you find another message. This time the message says: "May your best friend be well, may your best friend be happy."

You picture your best friend in your mind's eye and focus all your attention on him or her. You breathe deeply and the same golden radiance you felt before now spreads out to encircle your friend so that he or she is smiling back at you.

You climb still higher in the tree and read the next message. This time the message says: "May the person you like least be well, may he or she be happy.'"

The image of this person comes before you and he or she is smiling too. You realize that this is a person you care about and you're glad that he or she is happy and well.

You reach the highest point of the tree and the final message. It reads: "May all beings be well, may all beings be happy."

You look around you and see the deep, dense forest lying beneath you. All of the trees are rich with beautiful silver fruits that shine in the moonlight. You breathe deeply taking in the wonderful fragrance of the fruit hanging from every branch. You're glad to see so much beauty before you for every living thing to share.

Then you carefully climb back down the tree until you're safely on the ground once more.

Index of Values and Issues

These two complementary indexes cover the specific topics that the 18 stories of this book are designed to address directly or by implication. The same topics are covered from two different perspectives: positive (Values) and negative (Issues). Each index reference consists of an abbreviated story title, followed by the page number on which the story begins.

F
fear,
  of danger ahead,
    Aloka, 50
  of others,
    New Girl, 32
    Horse, 68
forgetfulness,
    Bella, 20
    Danan, 74
    Tim, 100

G
greed,
    Train, 40
    Monkey, 56
    Horse, 68
    Desert Willow, 106
    Antonio, 112

H
harming,
  ourselves,
    Danan, 74

I
injustice,
    Angelica, 62

L
laziness,

Sheep, 46
Egbert, 84

M
meanness,
    New Girl, 32
    Antonio, 112

N
naughtiness,
    Angelica, 62

O
obedience,
  lack of,
    Sheep, 46

S
selfishness,
    Moonlight Tree, 26
    Train, 40
    Antonio, 112
stealing,
    Train, 40
    Aloka, 50
    Monkey, 56
    Desert Willow, 106

T
temptation,
  giving into,

Train, 40
Monkey, 56
thoughtlessness,
    Train, 40
    Monkey, 56
    Egbert, 84

V
vanity,
    Monkey, 56
    Boar, 96
violence,
    Horse, 68

W
waste,
  of effort,
    Danan, 74
    Amrita, 90
worry, *see* anxiety

Acknowledgments

Inspiration comes in many forms and I want to thank the
following for their contributions to my life:

Urgen Sangharakshita, Atula, Aloka, Alvin Marcetti, Audrey Spowart,
Betty McMillan, Catherine Parkinson, Claire Kilmurry, Desmond Cheyne,
Elaine Black, Caterina O'Connor, Kuladharini, Lawrence McMillan,
Maitreyabandhu, Michael Kilmurry, Moksabandhu, Sahaja,
Stephen Potter, Suzanne Denis and Vimalacitta.

Note from the Author

If anything in this book is inaccurate, I ask forgiveness of my teachers – as well
as of my readers for having unwittingly impeded their way. As for what is accurate,
I hope the reader can use it, so that they may attain the truth to which it points.